ALMOST PERFECT

Linda Joy Singleton

D1352321

BANTAM BOOKS

NEW YORK • TORONTO • LONDON • SYDNEY • AUCKLAND

ALMOST PERFECT
A BANTAM BOOK 0 553 29445 2

First publication in Great Britain

PRINTING HISTORY
Bantam edition published 1993
Bantam edition reprinted 1995

Cover photo by Pat Hill

Bantam Books are published by Transworld Publishers Ltd, 61–63 Uxbridge Road, Ealing, London W5 5SA, in Australia by Transworld Publishers (Australia) Pty Ltd, 15–25 Helles Avenue, Moorebank, NSW 2170, and in New Zealand by Transworld Publishers (NZ) Ltd, 3 William Pickering Drive, Albany, Auckland.

Printed and bound in Great Britain by Cox & Wyman Ltd, Reading, Berkshire.

*With special thanks to my
critique group of friends . . .
Eloise, Lynn, Kate, Robbie,
Nan, Barbara, and Barbara*

Chapter One

"You want a bucket of seaweed and a sand dollar?" I asked my grandmother.

Lenora nodded. "That's right, Serena. Oh, and don't forget to bring me some seashells, too. Assorted colors would be nice—pink, white, coral, and gray," she added, tucking a snowy strand of hair underneath her floppy yellow hat.

Seaweed, seashells, and a sand dollar? I sighed. I should be used to my grandmother's odd requests by now. Lenora was a wood-sculpture artist, and the residents of Sea Mist considered her a bit eccentric. As one of these residents, I knew from experience that

1

my grandmother was more than just a *bit* eccentric. Still, I admired her creativity and loved her dearly.

"The seashells and seaweed will be easy to find," I said as I rose from a wicker chair, "but I don't know about the sand dollar. Usually I can only find broken pieces. Won't a half-dollar do?" I asked, wondering what kind of creation Lenora planned to make this time. Probably the strangest ever, which meant some trendy tourist would call it modern art and pay an outrageous amount for it.

Lenora smiled and shook her head, which made the flower on top of her hat flip-flop back and forth. "Serena dear, I need a *whole* sand dollar—nothing less. You're such a wonderful swimmer, I know you can find one for me."

"But a *perfect* sand dollar?" I countered, twisting the end of my long braid. "It's almost impossible!"

"Not for my granddaughter," Lenora replied. "You're a splendid swimmer. Only the dolphins swim better than you do."

"What do you mean *better*?" I asked teasingly. "I can keep up with any dolphin!"

Lenora laughed. "You probably can. Sometimes I think you're half fish and half girl.

You spend more time in the water than you do on land."

"Only because you're always sending me on treasure hunts. It's a good thing I'm not tied down to school activities, or else you'd have to find your sea treasures yourself," I said, wrapping a blue beach towel around my waist and slipping a pair of goggles around my neck.

Lenora patted my hand fondly. "I'd be the first one to applaud if you took part in a few activities. Sometimes I worry about you, Serena. At your age I had lots of school friends—and even a boyfriend or two," she added, her dark eyes twinkling with mischief.

I snorted. "A boyfriend! Forget it. That may have been okay for you, but not for me. I don't have anything in common with the kids at school."

"Maybe that's because you don't give them a chance."

"I'd give them a chance if they really wanted one," I told her. "But the other kids don't understand me, and I don't care. I like things just the way they are. I'd much rather spend my time at home and in the ocean."

"Well, I won't deny I'm glad to have you

here," Lenora said, maneuvering me toward the door. "Especially when I need things for my sculptures. You're so resourceful when it comes to locating hard-to-find objects."

"Like perfect sand dollars?" I asked with a knowing grin. "You're trying to sweet-talk me, Lenora, and it's working. I'll find those treasures for you if it takes all day."

"Splendid! I knew I could count on you," Lenora said, opening the screen door for me. "Now hurry along. I'm eager to begin my sculpture, but I won't be able to until you return."

I kissed my grandmother on the cheek, then stepped outside.

Immediately my senses were filled with salty sea breezes and the sounds of crying sea gulls. The sun peeked through a marsh-mallowy cloud, and the ocean waves were calm and gentle. It was going to be a beautiful day.

I took a breath of crisp air and grinned to myself. Springtime in Southern California was wonderful. A feeling of joy soared through me, and I felt like skipping and jumping across the sand.

But just as suddenly as the joyous feeling came it disappeared, replaced with a stab of

4

melancholy. I couldn't skip or jump—at least not without effort. A car accident three years ago, when I was thirteen, had changed all that—and so much more. I might be able to swim like a fish in the water, but on land all I could do was limp.

I glanced down at my right leg. Skin grafts had dimmed the scars below my knee, but they still looked red and ugly to me. They were a reminder that my parents were gone forever, killed in that same car crash. Also gone were my long-ago hopes of becoming an Olympic swimmer. A year of physical therapy had given me back most of my swimming skills, but not enough. While I was a better-than-average swimmer, I would never be a "star."

I gritted my teeth and purposely looked away from my scarred leg. Today was too nice a day to waste another minute indulging in self-pity. I gazed out at the Pacific Ocean, and a soothing calm filled me. Something about the ocean had always touched my heart and eased my pain.

I hurried to the shore and waded into the surf. When the water reached my thighs I pushed my goggles up over my eyes and dove in.

The water felt great, cool and refreshing. I splashed around, enjoying the buoyant freedom it gave to my legs. I could leap and dance in the water as I never could on land.

I wondered if any of my animal friends would show up today. Over the years I'd made friends with three sea gulls, a couple of sea lions, and even a dolphin. The dolphin was my favorite. When I first met the dolphin, I couldn't determine its gender, so I just assumed it was a boy. I nicknamed him Twinkie because of the white band around his middle. Whenever he came around we would play together in the water.

Would he be in the cove today? I'd know soon enough, because the cove was the perfect place to search for Lenora's treasures.

With strong, swift strokes I swam around an outcropping of rocks, heading for the cove. It was a secret place for me—my own private beach. Its only access was from the sea or down a steep hillside, which was why it was mine alone. Few people swam in this area, and only a crazy person would attempt to hike down the overgrown cliff path.

So when I reached the cove and saw the

silhouette of somebody on the shore my first thought was, *That person must be crazy!*

My second and third thoughts were much different because, as I swam closer, I recognized the guy. His name was Sonny Sinclair, and he was a sophomore at Farringdon High, like me. Unlike me, though, he was very popular and outgoing. Sonny was the student council president and a part-time interviewer on a teen radio show for our local station, KNDE. He came from a wealthy family and lived in the biggest house in Sea Mist. All this and good looks, too! He had silky brown hair that curled around his ears, a tall, muscular build, and eyes as blue as the sea. I often heard girls at school sighing about what a hunk Sonny was, and I privately agreed with them.

I wasn't sure what to do now. I would have to go ashore to search for Lenora's sculpture necessities, but I didn't want to do it with Sonny there. While I tried to come to a decision, I rested a hand on a protruding rock and watched him. He wasn't totally alone. He had a tawny cocker spaniel with him, and the two were playing with a Frisbee.

Sonny spun the blue disk into the air over

and over, and the dog ran after it. They seemed to be having a terrific time. I found myself wishing I could be a part of it, but that was impossible, of course. While I knew who Sonny was, he wouldn't know who I was. If he recognized me at all, it would be because of my limp. It set me apart from the other kids at school, and I was sure they considered me an oddity.

Sonny's words traveled on the wind as he called to his dog.

"Ginger! Ginger, fetch!" Even his voice was appealing, I thought, and wondered what it would be like to have such a nice voice say my name.

Sonny spun the Frisbee into the sky again, this time higher than ever, so high that a breeze captured it and twirled it out over the water.

"Ginger," Sonny called. "Come on, girl! Fetch!" But the dog just backed away and lowered her head.

I giggled. Obviously, Ginger did not like the water.

Poor Sonny, I thought to myself. *He'll lose his Frisbee, unless he goes after it himself.* Which I doubted he would, because he was wearing jeans. Salt water–drenched jeans took forever to dry, and wearing them could be very uncomfortable.

"Fetch, Ginger! Get it, girl!" Sonny yelled again. His voice sounded frustrated.

I watched the blue disk float farther away from him. He would lose it for sure, unless someone helped him.

Maybe me?

But did I have the courage? Could shy, limping Serena actually talk to popular, handsome Sonny?

Before I knew it, I was swimming toward the Frisbee. When I reached it, I grabbed it and began swimming back to shore.

I stopped swimming when I was a few feet away from Sonny, careful to stay waist deep in the water. I might be brave enough to talk to him, but I certainly wasn't about to let him see the scars on my leg.

Sonny was clearly astonished to see me.

"Where did you come from?" he asked, catching the Frisbee when I tossed it to him.

"Uh—the sea," I said shyly. My heart was pounding furiously.

Sonny grinned. "Then you must be a mermaid. Although I didn't know mermaids wore swimsuits."

I couldn't resist teasing. "You try wearing

spiky seashells and itchy fish skins some-time. It can get very painful. I much prefer nylon."

"Very sensible," Sonny said, playing along. "But if you're really a mermaid, your hair shouldn't be in a braid. It should be loose and flowing."

"But long, loose hair would get in my eyes. I'd hate to bump into a hungry shark because I couldn't see where I was going. A tidy braid is much safer."

"Another sensible answer, Miss Mermaid," Sonny said, twirling his Frisbee on one finger. "But calling you Miss Mermaid seems too formal. What's your real name?"

"Serena," I answered, both relieved and disappointed he didn't recognize me from school.

"Serena," he echoed. "I like that. Serena, the siren of the sea. It suits you."

"I don't know about that," I said, lowering my gaze. "It's just a name."

"But I'll bet it belongs to you alone. Not like mine—I come from a long line of Sinclairs. I'm the fourth Edward Alexander Sinclair. My friends call me by my nickname. It's—"

"Sonny," I interrupted, then realized my error and slapped my hand over my mouth.

"Hey, you know my name!" Sonny exclaimed. "Have we met before?"

I shook my head, trying not to smile.

Sonny was studying my face. "There *is* something familiar about you. Where do you go to school?"

"Mermaids don't attend school with mere mortals," I said haughtily.

Sonny laughed. "All right, if you don't go to regular high school, where *do* you go? Does King Neptune have a special school for mermaids?"

"Of course! It's called H_2O High," I answered with a giggle. "That's where I learned to rescue lost Frisbees."

"Well, you obviously learned your lesson well. Thanks for rescuing mine. As you may have guessed," he added, reaching down to pet his dog, "Ginger doesn't like the water."

Ginger looked up at me and wagged her tail. "She's a sweet dog anyway," I said.

"She sure is," Sonny said. "And I think she likes you. She didn't growl at you like she usually does with people she doesn't know."

I twisted the end of my braid. "All animals seem to like me. I guess they know I like them."

"Why don't you come out of the water and

get to know Ginger better—and her owner?" Sonny suggested.

"*No!*" I cried, much too loudly. "I mean, I have things to do. That's why I came here, but I'd better go now."

Sonny started to come toward me, but the surf rolled forward and he stopped. "Hey, don't leave yet. I don't know anything about you. Where do you really go to school? Where do you live? What's your last name?"

Without answering, I turned around and dove into the water. Swimming faster than ever, I left the cove. I would come back later to find shells and a sand dollar for Lenora. Being with Sonny was too confusing; both wonderful and painful. Wonderful because he was a special boy—the kind of boy I might have dated if I were popular and normal— and painful because I *wasn't* popular and normal. I was the class freak, and that's the way it would always be.

If only I were really a mermaid. Or as Sonny had teasingly called me, "a siren of the sea."

If only . . .

Chapter Two

On the way to school Monday morning, I stared out the car window while Lenora talked nonstop about her newest driftwood sculpture.

". . . And the sand dollar will be in the center with dried seaweed surrounding it. I see this piece as the expression of the harmony of the universe, an artist's view of the earth and the ocean. It will be unique and exquisite. That sand dollar you found for me is the perfect touch," Lenora said excitedly as she turned the car into the high school parking lot.

"Uh-huh," I said absently. My mind continued to wander, and I was only half hearing my grandmother. For some weird reason I kept seeing images of Sonny Sinclair at the cove. I just couldn't forget him.

But thinking about Sonny was useless, I reminded myself. Yesterday's meeting had been wonderful—like a dream—but today I would have to face reality. School was reality. And at school, I was nobody.

The car came to a stop and I climbed out. I kissed Lenora good-bye, and then headed for my first class. As I walked up the steps my right leg throbbed, so I walked more slowly and forced my legs to move naturally. Perhaps it was my imagination, but I felt the other kids' eyes on me.

This feeling of being watched continued through my first-period English class. While tall, slow-speaking Mr. Swaine discussed the works of Charles Dickens I had trouble paying attention. Someone was staring at me—I could sense it.

I glanced around the room, first to the left and then to the right. Nothing unusual—just the typical half-asleep kids and bored doodlers. So I pretended to drop a pen and looked behind me.

A pretty brown-haired girl met my gaze and smiled. I'd never exchanged more than a few words with her, but I knew who she was.

Diane Christensen—student council secretary, yearbook chairman, and the prettiest girl at Farringdon. Had she been the one watching me? If so, why?

Immediately I felt self-conscious. Was the tag sticking out of the neck of my blouse? Had someone placed a "kick me" sign on my back?

As I was puzzling over these possibilities, I felt a light tap on my shoulder and heard a whispered "Here."

"Huh?" I murmured, turning slightly to look at Diane.

"Take the note," she said.

Confused, I reached back and took the piece of paper she handed me. Slowly, I unfolded it.

Serena,
You're probably surprised I'm writing to you. I don't know you very well, but I know your name. Would you like to eat lunch with my friends and me today?
There's something important I want to ask you.

See ya then!
Diane

Diane was right when she guessed I'd be surprised to hear from her. I wondered what she wanted to ask me. Maybe she needed help studying for our upcoming English test. Yeah, that made sense. I always got straight As in English. Then again, maybe Diane's lunch invitation had nothing to do with schoolwork. But what else could she possibly want to talk about?

For the rest of the period I tried to pay attention to Mr. Swaine's lecture, but I couldn't concentrate. Finally, the bell rang.

I stood up quickly and turned around. "Diane," I said, "I—uh—I read your note."

Diane smiled, and I noticed how beautiful she was with her sky-blue eyes, creamy complexion, and elegant features. She wore a yellow miniskirt and a green-and-beige cotton blouse. I glanced at my own faded jeans, knowing I would never dare to show my legs in a short skirt.

"Can you make it?" Diane asked. "I'd really like to talk to you."

I tightened my grip on my books. "I don't know. Your friends might not like me joining you for lunch," I said shyly as we started walking out of the room.

"They'd be glad to have you."

I gnawed on my lower lip. The idea of having lunch with Diane's popular crowd made me uncomfortable. "Can't we just talk now?"

"There isn't enough time," Diane replied. "I want to explain the whole situation before I spring it on you."

"I don't understand. . . ."

"Of course you don't," Diane said with a chuckle. "Not yet, anyway. But I promise to tell you everything later. I know we've never talked much before, but I knew you must be the one."

"The one?" I was more puzzled than ever.

Diane nodded. "Yes. Not too many girls have an unusual name like Serena. I wish I had a name like that. Diane's okay, but it's ordinary. Why, there must be at least three other Dianes at Farringdon High."

"Diane's a very pretty name."

She grinned. "You really *are* nice. I always thought you were, even though you're so quiet. I've always been kind of afraid to talk to you, but I wish I had. I'd bet we'd be great friends by now."

I smiled a little. "I—I don't have many friends. I mean, I'm kind of a loner."

"Really? I'm *never* alone, and sometimes I wish I were. I'm always so busy. Student council meetings, yearbook meetings, baby-sitting, swimming practice—I never have a minute to myself."

A glance at my watch made me worry I'd be late for my next class. "I really have to go to my locker," I said. "About lunch—well, I don't usually eat in the cafeteria. I don't much like crowds and noise. Maybe we could meet outside."

"Outside? Great idea! Okay, I'll meet you there. And after you listen to my idea, be prepared to say yes. Uh-oh—there's the bell! Gotta run! See you later!"

I was glad I hadn't agreed to sit with Diane's friends. She was awfully sweet, but her best friend, Pamela Thorne, had a reputation for being outspoken and pushy. I often wondered why the two hung out together. While Diane was gentle as a kitten, Pamela was like a crouching tigress—you never knew when she'd pounce.

As I headed for my own class, I was even more curious about what Diane was going to ask me. Maybe to help with the yearbook or to be on a school committee? Or maybe like I'd originally thought—something to do with English.

Whatever it was, I'd find out in a few hours.

I was sitting under my favorite willow tree and had just taken a bite of my apple when I heard footsteps behind me.

"Diane?" I said as I started to turn around. "I've been waiting . . ."

My words trailed off as I saw that the blue eyes looking down at me didn't belong to Diane.

I gasped. "Sonny! What are you doing here?"

Sonny sat down on the grass next to me. "I hope you're not disappointed. I could leave if you want me to," he said with a grin.

"No!" I exclaimed, and then flushed with embarrassment. "I mean, there's no reason for you to leave. It's—uh—nice to see you again."

"Nice to see you, too. I'm relieved to see you have legs instead of a fish's tail."

"That's because I'm only a mermaid on weekends," I said, glad I was wearing jeans so Sonny couldn't see my scars.

"Why didn't you tell me you went to Farringdon High?" he asked. "I figured you were a

19

tourist or something, and I'd never see you again. All I knew was that your name was Serena. Boy, was I surprised when a friend of mine recognized your name."

I felt thrilled beyond belief. Sonny Sinclair had been asking about me!

"You disappeared into the ocean so quickly I was beginning to think you might really be a mermaid," he went on.

"My grandmother says I'm part fish. Doesn't that make me a mermaid?"

He chuckled. "Maybe. And even if you're not a mermaid, you're a terrific swimmer. Where did you learn to swim so well?"

"I could swim before I could walk," I answered. "I swam competitively for a community team, and then my parents enrolled me in advanced classes."

"You must have wonderful parents."

"I did," I said. "They died in a car accident when I was thirteen. I was in the car, too, but I was luckier than they were. I only injured my leg."

"Oh," Sonny said. "I'm sorry."

"It's okay," I said quickly. "My memories of my parents are all happy ones. Now I live with my grandmother."

"Is your grandmother a swimmer, too?"

I giggled. "No way! Lenora says salt water ruins the complexion. She always wears huge hats, and she never even wades in the ocean."

"She sounds interesting. I'd like to meet her someday," Sonny said.

"That's easy enough. She owns the Unique Creations Boutique on the wharf, and she's almost always there. I work there, too, sometimes."

Sonny put his hand over mine, and smiled brightly. My heart raced and my mind spun. Was Sonny actually flirting with me?

Before he could say anything more, Diane arrived. "Sorry I'm late," she said, out of breath. "Pam insisted I eat lunch with her and the gang. I hurried, but maybe I didn't need to." She grinned at Sonny. "She *is* your mermaid, isn't she?"

Sonny let go of my hand and smiled. "Right on target, Diane. I owe you one."

"I *knew* it!" Diane said, sitting down next to us. "Serena is such a distinctive name. There couldn't be two of them in a town this size."

I frowned in puzzlement. "Am I missing something? What are you two talking about?"

"You!" Diane answered with a giggle.

"Diane's the one who recognized your name," Sonny explained. "We were talking on the phone last night, and I mentioned meeting a mysterious mermaid named Serena."

"He told me how you saved his Frisbee, and what a fantastic swimmer you are," Diane said.

I blushed. "I don't know about 'fantastic,' but I do love to swim."

"Just how much?" Diane asked, looking at me intently.

"I love swimming more than anything, I guess."

"Super! That's just what I wanted to hear," Diane exclaimed.

"Why?" I asked.

Diane suddenly looked nervous. She turned to Sonny. "*You* ask her, okay? You explain things better than I do."

He flashed her an amused look, then turned to me. "When I told Diane how impressed I was with your swimming skill, she got really excited. Diane's on the girls' swim team and one of the members just moved away. The team needs a new swimmer, and I think you'd be perfect."

"Me? On the girls' swim team?" I almost choked. Everyone would see my legs!

Sonny grinned. "That's the idea."

"Can you try out today?" Diane asked hopefully.

I thought of an easy excuse. "I don't have a swimsuit here."

"No problem," Diane replied. "I have an extra, and I'm sure it'll fit you."

Sonny reached for my hand again and grinned. "So how about it, Serena? The team really needs a good swimmer. Will you try out?"

Every fiber of my brain screamed out for me to say no. I'd be too embarrassed. People would point at me and laugh. I just couldn't do it!

But when I looked up into Sonny's sea-blue eyes, my brain grew fuzzy. My mouth opened, ready to say the word *no*.

But I couldn't. Instead, I said, "Yes."

Chapter Three

The minute Diane and Sonny left, I realized that I had made a big mistake. I was a basket case for the rest of the school day. When the last bell rang, I decided I just couldn't go through with it. I'd simply take the bus home as usual and pretend that today was no different than any other day.

But when I reached my locker, Diane was waiting for me. "Ready to try out for the team?" she said.

I bit my lip. "I—I don't know. . . . I'll miss my bus."

"No problem. I'll give you a lift home afterward. When I turned sixteen last month my folks surprised me with a gorgeous green Camaro."

"Your own car?" I asked, awed. "Wow! I've been saving for a car for years, but at the rate I'm going I'll get gray hair before I get a car."

Diane laughed. "Don't worry. You might get lucky and turn prematurely gray."

I smiled a little, then sighed. "I—uh—don't know about joining the swim team. I really don't think it's a good idea."

"Why not?" Diane asked with genuine surprise. "I'm sure you'll do great."

"That's not the problem," I said slowly, touching my right leg. "Haven't you noticed anything *different* about me?"

"Well, you're a little shy. . . ."

I sighed again, impatiently. "Are you just being kind or something? Everyone knows I'm Farringdon High's resident cripple."

"Oh, you mean your limp," Diane said matter-of-factly.

"You *have* noticed it," I said. "Then you understand why I can't join the swim team."

"Are you serious?" Diane asked incredulously. "You really think people care about that? Get real, Serena! Nobody cares about how you walk."

"Sure they do. I catch kids staring at me all the time. They either think I'm weird or they feel sorry for me."

"I'm amazed you actually believe that," Diane said, shaking her head. "Well, you're wrong. And I intend to prove it."

"How?"

"Come with me and try out for the team. If you're a good swimmer, you'll make it. Our coach, Barbara, is fair and smart. How you walk on land won't matter one bit if you're good in the water."

Diane's words challenged me, and I said, "Okay, I'll do it."

"Good!" she said, grabbing my arm. "Then let's go! We don't want to be late."

I nodded, feeling excited despite my fears. I must have missed competitive swimming more than I'd realized. Thank goodness Diane had stopped me from running away—I hate cowards almost as much as I hate being pitied. And maybe I'd actually make the team. If so, my life would change. I'd be part of a group. I'd have new friends—maybe good, close friends, like Diane and Sonny.

Sonny. Just thinking about him made me feel warm inside. He was so handsome and considerate. He'd be a wonderful boyfriend. I envied the lucky girl who captured his heart. I wondered if I could be that lucky. . . .

Then a terrible thought struck me—Sonny might already have a girlfriend! Why hadn't I thought of that before? He wasn't the kind of guy girls left alone. But did he care about any special girl?

And if Sonny *didn't* have a girl, did that mean I had a chance? Was it possible for him to like *me*? Maybe not the shy, brainy Serena who was a nobody, but the shy, brainy Serena who was the star of the swim team.

Going out for the swim team could be the best thing that ever happened to me, I decided, especially where Sonny Sinclair was concerned.

"See? My suit fits you perfectly," Diane said, smiling at me. "And here's a swimming cap. With all that hair, you'll definitely need one."

I made a face at the cap, but obediently put it on.

"You look great, Serena. Are you ready?"

"I guess," I said, my stomach knotting up with sudden nervousness. "But I wish I could keep this towel wrapped around my legs because of the scars. I'm not used to swimming where there are lots of people."

"There won't be lots of people—less than a dozen. And your scars are hardly noticeable. Just relax and have fun. You'll do fine."

"I hope so," I murmured as I followed Diane out of the locker room.

The sight of the swimming pool sparkling in the afternoon sun gave me strength. Eight or nine girls were doing warm-up exercises. A young woman—probably the coach, I figured—was speaking to them. She waved when she caught sight of Diane and me.

"There you are, Diane. And this must be Serena."

I smiled shyly. "Hi. I guess I'm here to try out for the team."

"Welcome, Serena. I'm the coach, Barbara Dale," she said, extending her hand and smiling warmly at me. "Diane tells me you're used to swimming in the ocean."

I nodded. "I swim every day."

"Just what a coach likes to hear. If you join the team, you'll have to practice every afternoon. Ten grueling hours a week, plus some weekends. Can you handle that?"

"Yes," I answered truthfully. "And I'll try my best. I mean, I honestly love swimming."

"Good. Why don't you join the team for warm-ups, then we'll check out your strokes."

I nodded and positioned myself next to Diane for warm-ups. Nobody even glanced at my bad leg. My confidence was rising, and I felt pretty good.

Soon Barbara was leading me over to the deep end of the pool. Out of the corner of my eye, I noticed Diane giving me the thumbs-up signal. It was try-out time!

At Barbara's request, I dove into the water and began with a simple freestyle fifty meter. I demonstrated the backstroke, the breast-stroke, the butterfly, and more—my years of training hadn't been for nothing. I instinctively knew I was performing well.

When I had finished, Barbara was clearly pleased.

"Where have you been hiding, Serena? You should have joined the team when you were a freshman," she said, handing me a towel.

"Does this mean I made it?" I asked, reaching up to take off my cap.

"Definitely," Barbara said with enthusiasm. "You more than made it. It's too soon to tell, but I think you have the potential to be a lead swimmer."

"Really?" I said, feeling a surge of happiness that almost made me light-headed.

She nodded. "Yes, really. Let me be the first to welcome you to the team."

When Barbara announced to the team that I was their new member, Diane's reaction was super. "Yay!" she cheered and applauded.

"Glad to have you," a tall, dark-skinned girl named Andrea said. "Your swimming was pretty awesome."

"You're just what we need to win the regional meet," a short, blond girl named Tara added enthusiastically.

I grinned. All this praise, and not one word about my scarred leg. My worrying had been for nothing.

For the remaining two hours I enjoyed swimming with the team. I was doing well with most of the strokes. The freestyle was my best and the breaststroke my weakest. I was faster and stronger than the others— my only real competition was Diane's best friend, Pamela Thorne.

When practice was over, I went back to the locker room with Diane. Noisy, happy voices echoed off the walls as the girls showered and changed out of their wet swimsuits.

Ten minutes later Diane and I were walking toward her car. It was easy to spot—the green Camaro with the good-looking boy standing next to it.

"Sonny!" I cried out. "I'm so glad to see you! I made the team!"

Sonny grinned at me. "I'm not surprised. I knew my favorite mermaid could make it."

That made me blush. I loved the idea of being Sonny's "favorite" anything!

Diane unlocked her car door. "Serena, I guess I forgot to mention Sonny and I share rides to school sometimes. Who drives depends on our schedules. Today it's my turn."

"I hope taking me home isn't a problem. If it is—" I began, but Sonny interrupted.

"No problem at all," he said. "Besides, I have an ulterior motive. I want to find out where you live, so the next time you vanish into the ocean, I'll know where to find you."

Sonny was definitely acting as if he liked me, and I was thrilled. I hadn't had a boy interested in me since I was thirteen—right before the accident. And after the accident, the only thing Jon Andersen felt for me was pity. My romantic hopes had quickly disappeared.

A sudden shout broke into my thoughts. Somebody was calling Diane's name. I immediately recognized Pamela Thorne, the only person who hadn't welcomed me to the swim team.

Diane smiled at Pamela. "Hi, Pam. What's up?"

"Car trouble again?" Sonny asked.

Pamela shook her head and spoke directly to Diane and Sonny, ignoring me. "No, nothing like that. I'm glad I caught you two in time. We're having an emergency meeting of the student council at my house in an hour."

"What's the rush?" Sonny asked, clearly annoyed.

"It's about next weekend's Spring Fling dance. The band just canceled," Pamela said.

"What?" Diane exclaimed. "But we don't have enough time to find another band!"

"We have to do something. That's why I called this meeting. You both can make it, can't you?" Pam asked.

"We'll be there," Diane promised, and Sonny nodded. "All I have to do is take Serena home, then Sonny and I'll go right to your place." She finally realized that Pamela and I hadn't spoken. "Pam, you've met Serena, right?"

Pamela shrugged. "Not exactly, but I know who she is."

I smiled at her. "I saw you swim today. You're really good."

"That's why I'm the team's lead swimmer," Pamela said. Her expression was far from friendly. Did she know that Barbara was considering me for lead swimmer? She raised an eyebrow at me and said sweetly, "Did you know we share the same P.E. period, Serena?"

"Huh?" That was news to me.

"Oh, I guess you wouldn't know. You don't take *regular* P.E., like the rest of us. You're in that *special* class."

The familiar feeling of embarrassment washed over me. I couldn't take regular P.E. because of my limp. Sports like soccer, softball, and track were much too difficult.

"Cut it out, Pam," Sonny snapped, slipping a protective arm around my shoulders. "I know you're upset about the band canceling, but that's no reason to be nasty to Serena."

"Sonny and I will be at the meeting," Diane said quickly, obviously feeling awkward. After all, Pamela had been her friend for a long time and I'd only been her friend for one day.

"Good," Pamela said. "And don't forget to let me know what colors you're both wearing to the Spring Fling dance. I'm ordering corsages and boutonnieres for all student council members."

"I already told you," Diane said, sounding a little exasperated. "Sonny's wearing navy blue and I'm wearing green. And *please* don't remind us to be at the dance early. We're already planning to get there at six o'clock."

Pamela nodded, but her eyes were gazing at me, sending me a message.

With a heavy heart, I knew what the message was. Why hadn't I realized it before? There *was* a special girl in Sonny's life, and she'd been under my nose the whole time.

Diane.

Sonny and Diane. They were more than friends. They were a couple.

Chapter Four

Sitting on a rock very early the next morning, surrounded by churning blue waters, I threw a red plastic ball into the air. The ball soared high and then fell. Suddenly a sleek, silver-gray creature burst out of the water and bounced the ball back into the air directly toward me.

I laughed as I caught it.

"Good shot, Twinkie!" I called with delight. "You did it again, boy. You must have the fastest nose in the West—for a dolphin, that is!"

Twinkie hit the water with one flipper and made a shrill sound that reminded me of a high-pitched giggle. Then he splashed and seemed to dance backward on his tail.

"You still want to play catch?" I asked.

Twinkie splashed some more and made a clicking sound.

Taking that as a *yes*, I tossed the ball to him again. As before, he sprang like a shimmering missile out of the water and boomeranged the ball back to me.

I smiled. Playing with Twinkie this morning was the perfect tonic for my aching heart. He was a loyal friend who would listen.

"Here you go again," I said, tossing the ball farther and higher than before. "Catch!"

Seconds later, the ball was once again in my hands. I never ceased to be amazed by how intelligent Twinkie was. He acted like a playful child, yet he stared at me with such wise eyes. No wonder some people considered dolphins the second most intelligent animals. Naturally, humans were considered the first—but the way I was feeling right now, I felt I was anything *but* intelligent. In fact, I felt downright foolish.

Just how serious were Sonny and Diane about each other? I wondered. They didn't act lovey-dovey, or even hold hands. But they *were* going to the Spring Fling dance together.

I stood up on the rock and hurled the ball onto the shore. Then I slumped back down and sighed.

"Why did Sonny act as if he was interested in me, when he's dating Diane?" I asked Twinkie.

The dolphin obviously didn't know the answer to this question any more than I did.

"I'm just so confused." I sighed, gathering my wet hair in one hand and flinging it over my shoulder. "I really like Sonny more than I've ever liked a boy—and I know it isn't just a crush. All I could dream about last night was him. We danced together, we splashed in the water, and we even kissed. It was so wonderful, like it was meant to be. But then I woke up and had a reality attack. How could I possibly dream about another girl's guy? Especially when the girl is Diane—one of the sweetest, kindest people I've ever met." My shoulders sagged. "Maybe I'll skip school today."

Twinkie yapped and squeaked, then glided in the shallow water until his smooth, leathery nose touched the bottom of my foot.

"Oooh! That tickles," I squealed, slipping off the rock with a splash and joining the dolphin in the water. "You rat! I'll get you!"

Images of Sonny and Diane fled from my mind as I swam after Twinkie. Playing with him always lifted my spirits. Winning his trust hadn't been easy, but after a year of bribing him with fishy snacks we were the best of buddies.

Of course, having a dolphin for a friend wasn't like owning a dog or a cat. Twinkie only showed up occasionally, and he was often gone for weeks at a time. I always assumed that was when he was out playing games with lovely female dolphins. He could probably teach me a few things about the mating game, I thought.

A glance at the rising sun made me leave Twinkie and head for the house. Lenora was probably waking up by now. She was used to my morning swims, so she wouldn't wonder where I was. Still, I didn't want to keep Lenora waiting, especially since it was my turn to fix breakfast.

I hurried into the house and changed out of my wet swimsuit. My earlier idea of skipping school was tempting, but there was no way I would actually do it. Skipping school meant skipping the opportunity to be near Sonny, and I couldn't bear the thought of not seeing him today.

School was tolerable, but I felt lonely because both Sonny and Diane were involved with committee projects between classes, and I barely had a chance to talk to them. It was probably better that way, I told myself.

But as the day progressed I realized I was genuinely looking forward to swimming practice. Diane met me at my locker again, only this time she didn't have to convince me to go with her. In fact, I hurried into the girls' locker room, slipped out of my regular clothes, and changed into my blue-striped swimsuit before Diane had even taken off her shoes. I couldn't wait to hit the water!

My swimming times were even better today. Barbara complimented me more than once, mentioning again that I was lead-swimmer material. Pamela Thorne happened to be nearby when she said that, and from then on every time I glanced at Pamela she was glaring at me. I tried to ignore her, but ignoring Pamela was difficult. She constantly found excuses for private chats with Diane. And whenever they whispered, I wondered what they were talking about—school, swimming, or *me*?

When practice was over, Diane and I walked to her car. It would be just the two of us today, since Sonny worked at the radio station after school on Tuesdays and Thursdays. I was both disappointed and relieved not to see Sonny. I would have loved to be near him, but I knew it wasn't right.

"Do you mind if I tune in KNDE?" Diane asked, reaching for the radio as she started up the engine. "I love to listen to Sonny—his 'Teen Scene' show is super. Today he's interviewing the president of the school science club. I don't know anything about science, but Melvin Engeldinger has such a cute smile."

"Melvin *what*?"

"Engeldinger," Diane repeated with a giggle. "He's in my biology class, and I swear he's smarter than the teacher. It was my idea for Sonny to interview him. Sonny's job is so exciting," she went on enthusiastically. "I've been to the station, and it's terrific. You should go sometime."

"I wouldn't want to impose," I said, feeling uncomfortable.

"Don't be silly. Sonny would love to show you around. Or even better, he could interview you. Farringdon's newest swimming star!"

"No way!" I cried, blushing. "I may swim okay, but I'm nothing special. I hate the idea of drawing attention to myself."

"You're too modest," Diane said, adjusting her rearview mirror. "And you *are* special. You're pretty, a fabulous swimmer, and an A student. You can be anything you want to be."

I couldn't resist a smile. "Diane, you're going to give me a swelled head! I've never thought of myself as anything but ordinary. Though sometimes I daydream about becoming a marine biologist," I admitted.

"You mean studying the ocean and seaweed and stuff?" Diane asked.

"Something like that. Mainly I want to learn more about dolphins. They fascinate me—I've read a lot about them. I've even made friends with one. I call him Twinkie, and he's incredibly smart."

"Maybe Melvin Engeldinger was a dolphin in another life," Diane said with a grin, stopping for a red light. "Oh, listen!" she exclaimed, turning the volume up. "Sonny's on. He's introducing Melvin!"

". . . Engeldinger, Farringdon High's hotshot scientist. Remember his name, because years from now he's sure to win a Nobel prize," Sonny was saying. "Tell us about yourself, Melvin."

"I'd be glad to," Melvin replied. "My interest in science began when I received my first chemistry set. If I remember correctly, I was four."

Traffic noises outside faded away while Diane and I listened to Melvin talk about his love for science. He sounded stiff and a bit shy. I guess he was nervous, and I could sympathize with that. Talking on the radio would scare me, too.

Soon Diane had turned down the street leading to my home.

"Isn't he wonderful?" Diane asked eagerly.

"Sonny or Melvin?" I teased. I was sure she meant Sonny, and I couldn't agree with her more. I only wished I didn't feel so jealous of Diane's relationship with him.

"Both of them, I guess," Diane said, blushing. "Melvin's such a brain, and Sonny does a great job of interviewing."

"Yeah," I replied as Diane pulled into my driveway, "he's good all right. One day he'll probably be famous."

Diane shook her head. "No way. He's going

into banking like his dad. Sonny's future is all arranged by his parents. *Too* arranged, if you ask me, but Sonny doesn't talk about it much, so I'm not sure how he feels."

"I don't think I'd like having my life planned for me by other people," I said.

I invited Diane to come inside. I'd already told her a little about my grandmother, and Diane was eager to meet her.

We found Lenora in the living room. She was wearing a hat shaped like a bowl, decorated with plastic fruit. Lenora is the only person I know who wears a hat all the time, even in the house.

My grandmother grinned at Diane. "So you're the magician that convinced Serena to take up competitive swimming again! I don't know how you did it, but I'm grateful."

"Serena's a whiz in the water," Diane said. "Maybe the best swimmer on the team."

"My daughter, Serena's mother, was a talented swimmer, too. I'd say it runs in the family."

Diane smiled and looked around at the colorful paintings on the walls and the bizarre sculptures that were scattered about. "Your house is really attractive. I like all the artwork," she said.

"Don't decide so quickly whether you like it or not," Lenora told her. "*Absorb* the pieces. Do they make you feel an emotion? Do they touch your soul? That's the true measure of a piece of art."

Diane didn't say anything, and just stared at my grandmother. Lenora sometimes has that effect on people. Deciding that Diane needed rescuing, I made up a quick excuse and led her into my bedroom. My room was the one place in the house free of Lenora's personality. I had decorated it myself: three walls were painted turquoise and there was a delicate flower-patterned wallpaper on the fourth. I had twin beds, a dresser, a desk, and a crowded bookcase.

"Is it safe to say I like your room?" Diane asked, flashing me a teasing grin. "You won't give me a lecture on how to appreciate it, will you?"

I giggled and sat down on one of the beds. "Lenora takes a bit of getting used to. I love her dearly, but she can be overwhelming. She's not your typical grandmother. Just try not to mention art again, and you'll be fine."

Diane sat down on the other bed. "No problem. Instead of art talk, I'll bore her with student council or swim team highlights."

"Speaking of the student council, how did yesterday's meeting go?" I asked. "Did you find another band?"

"No, but Sonny convinced one of his pals from KNDE to be the deejay for the dance."

"Great idea," I said. Thinking that this might be a good time to find out how serious Diane and Sonny were about each other, I added, "I guess that means you and Sonny are still on for Saturday night."

"We sure are, and I'm relieved. I've already bought a fantastic dress to wear. It's the same shade of green as my car—the ultimate in color coordination!"

I took a deep breath and said, "It sounds awesome. So, I was wondering. About you and Sonny. Do you two go out often?"

Diane shrugged. "Our parents have been friends for years, so Sonny and I are always going places together. He's easy and fun to be with."

"I can tell," I said wistfully. "Doing things with someone like Sonny must be neat."

Diane looked at me sharply. "Serena, do you like Sonny?"

"Of course not!" I lied. "Sonny's *your* boyfriend."

Diane stared at me with astonishment. "No he isn't."

My mouth fell open. "But—but you're going to the Spring Fling dance together. . . . I don't understand," I said. "If you and Sonny aren't a couple—then what *are* you?"

"Very good friends," Diane answered cheerfully. "It's convenient for us to go out together, that's all. Neither of us has to worry about whether or not we'll have a date for some special occasion. It's great, but that doesn't mean there isn't room in our lives for one more friend. And if you're starting to like Sonny, then I have the perfect idea."

"What?"

Diane's blue eyes danced with excitement. "You have to go to the Spring Fling dance!"

"But I don't have a date—" I began.

"Yes you do!" Diane cried. "You can go to the dance with Sonny and me!"

Chapter Five

As generous as Diane's offer of a shared date had been, there was no way I could accept. If pride hadn't stopped me, my lack of dancing ability did. And though Diane tried hard to persuade me to change my mind, not even she could argue with a limp.

So on Saturday morning, while most of the girls at Farringdon High were getting beautified for the Spring Fling, I was pushing keys on a cash register at Unique Creations.

"That will be fifty-five dollars," I told the plump, orange-haired woman I was waiting on. I made change and carefully wrapped a seascape oil painting.

The woman thanked me, then disappeared through the glass doors. I sighed and thought to myself, *Saturday mornings are usually busier than this. Has everyone in town got Spring Fling fever?*

To pass the time I began rearranging some of the gift items on the shelves near the back of the store.

The jingle of the bell over the door, announcing another customer, made me jump and turn around. To my amazement, it was Sonny.

"Did I startle you?" he asked, smiling at me.

"A little," I admitted. "Can I—can I help you find something?"

"I've already found what I was looking for," he said in a breezy, friendly fashion. "You. I stopped by your house and your grandmother—Call-Me-Lenora—said you were here."

"You came to find me?" I asked, pleased but also puzzled. "Why?"

"To convince you to go to the dance with Diane and me tonight. Won't you change your mind?" he asked, lightly touching my arm.

I lowered my gaze. "I'd like to go, but I really can't."

"Why not?"

I glanced down at my right leg. "You must have noticed that I limp. I never go to dances. With my leg, dancing would be—awkward," I said uneasily.

"Oh, I never thought about that," Sonny said, sounding apologetic. "You're so amazing in the water, I forgot about your injury." He hesitated. "Well, if I can't see you tonight, how about this afternoon?"

I blinked. "What do you mean?"

Sonny grinned. "Your grandmother—excuse me, *Lenora*—said you were only covering for her until noon. So that means you're almost through. How about a beach picnic?"

"I'd love to," I murmured. "But are you sure you want to go with me?"

"Who else?" he retorted. "I have a weakness for mermaids, remember?"

"Well, I just thought that . . . I mean, I don't want to complicate things between you and Diane. I know she said you were just good friends, but . . ."

"We're *all* friends. And as a friend, I'm asking you to take pity on a lonely, hungry guy and share lunch with me. I can't think of a better combination than sun, surf, and Serena."

I was delighted by his invitation. "Well . . . all right. Yes, I'd love to go! But first I'd have to stop by my house and change," I said.

I just couldn't say no to Sonny. He was fun, considerate, and incredibly good-looking, and I was falling for him, head over heels.

I only hoped I wasn't making a big mistake.

An hour later we were finishing our picnic on the beach. "The chicken was delicious," I said, wiping my mouth with a paper napkin.

"I'll compliment the chef next time I go through the drive-up window," Sonny replied. "Not bad for an impromptu picnic."

"I completely agree," I said. "I'm stuffed. The water looks inviting, but if I went swimming now I'm sure I'd sink right to the bottom."

Sonny laughed. "Don't worry, I've been trained in life-saving procedures. I could always rescue you."

A mental image of myself in Sonny's strong arms sent a shiver up my spine. Almost drowning might just be worth it!

"Thanks for the offer, but I'll wait a while," I said, stretching out on my beach towel.

"Not a bad idea," Sonny said. "I'm ready to catch a few rays myself."

"You can tell me your life story while we relax," I suggested, propping myself up on one elbow and facing him.

He shrugged. "My life story's pretty boring. Give me twenty more years—then maybe I'll have something to talk about."

"Diane tells me you're going to go into banking some day," I prompted. "That sounds interesting."

"Not to me," Sonny said. "It's only interesting to people like my dad. I suppose I'll get used to it, though. Dad's always saying banking is in my blood."

"You don't sound very thrilled about the idea," I commented.

"Probably because I'm not. It's hard to picture myself in a business suit juggling stocks, bonds, and dollars. But I guess that's what I'll be doing."

"Why? Because your family expects it?"

"You got it," Sonny answered. "The men in my family have always been bankers, and the pressure's really on, because I'm an only child. Dad's counting on me."

I studied Sonny's serious expression. It was obvious to me he wasn't happy with his ready-made career, so I tried to cheer him up. "Hey, I listened to all your radio shows this week," I said. "Tuesday's show was especially great. You did a super job interviewing Melvin Engeldinger."

Sonny's face lit up. "Thanks! I really love working at KNDE. Broadcasting has got to be the most exciting profession in the world."

"The station's lucky to have you," I said sincerely. "You're really good."

"You couldn't give me a better compliment," Sonny said. "That job means a lot to me. When I'm at KNDE, I'm not Edward Alexander Sinclair the Fourth. I'm just Sonny."

"Sonny Sinclair!" I announced, pretending to talk into an invisible microphone. "KNDE's hottest radio personality!"

"Yes, folks," Sonny joined in, taking my make-believe mike. "Today you're in for a big treat. *Two* major talents destined for mega-stardom! It's Sonny on the air and Serena in the water!"

I jumped up. "Did you say water? Time to hit the surf! Last one in is a slimy jellyfish!"

Laughing, I waded into the ocean and then dove through a wave. When I came up for breath, I saw Sonny waving at me from the shore.

"You win," he called. "I'm a slimy jellyfish!"

"Hey, come on in," I shouted. "The water's great!"

Sonny shook his head. "Not yet. The sun feels too good."

"You lazy beach bum!" I yelled.

Sonny just smiled, then stretched out on his towel.

The water felt too wonderful for me to even consider returning to shore so soon.

I swam deeper into the sea, alternating from an energetic freestyle to a relaxing backstroke. I'd only been on the swim team for a week, but I could already feel how much stronger my strokes had become. I felt terrific!

After ten minutes or so, I started to head back to land, but a shrill sound nearby made me turn around. It was Twinkie.

"Hi fella," I said, paddling next to him and stroking his smooth skin. "How ya doing, pretty boy?"

He shook his nose and made a clicking noise.

"Pretty good, huh? Well, I can't play very long today. See that hunky guy on the beach?" I whispered to the dolphin. "I'm with him— at least for this afternoon. Tonight he has a date with another girl."

Twinkie slapped one flipper against the water and cackled his high-pitched laugh.

"So you think that's funny, do you?" I asked with mock sternness. I enjoyed pretending that Twinkie could actually understand human conversation.

Twinkie splashed and flipped his tail. He didn't want to talk—he wanted to play. So I grabbed hold of his dorsal fin and swam with him. When he dove I tried to follow, but I had to resurface before he did. Then he came up suddenly, showering me with spray. He glided forward and playfully circled me, his dorsal fin all I could see.

From the shore, I heard someone call my name.

Looking around, I saw Sonny dashing wildly into the surf.

Puzzled, I watched as he took long, strong strokes toward me. What was he so excited about?

"Serena!" Sonny called as he swam. "Watch out! *Shark!*"

Alarm spread through me. Had he said *shark*?

Now Sonny was less than ten yards from me, zipping through the water like a missile. Again I heard him yell, "Shark!"

I looked around for the ominous sight of a shark fin, but all I saw were the ocean, Twinkie, and Sonny. More confused than afraid, I started swimming toward Sonny.

"Serena!" he exclaimed, breathing hard. He reached out, wrapping his strong arms around me. "We have to get out of here! Don't you see it? It's a shark!"

My gaze followed where Sonny's finger was pointing, and I started laughing.

"It's not a shark!" I swallowed water and laughed even harder. "That's a dolphin!"

Sonny's face registered shock and amazement. "A *dolphin*? But the fin—it looked like a shark's!"

"You've been watching too many *Jaws* movies. This dolphin is my friend. His name's Twinkie."

"Twinkie?" Sonny echoed, still holding me as we both treaded water.

"I call him that because of the white band around his middle," I explained.

With great timing, the dolphin splashed behind us and made his crazy cackling noise.

"You must think I'm a first-class bozo," Sonny said, "mistaking a dolphin for a shark."

I smiled. "Not a bozo—a wonderfully brave

person. You tried to save me, even though you thought Twinkie was a shark. You're a real hero!"

"But he wasn't a shark," Sonny mumbled.

"You didn't know that," I said, looking up into his eyes. "I'm flattered that you were worried about me."

We had drifted closer to shore now, and our feet touched the bottom. He held me closer and gazed at me. "Worried?" he echoed. "Try terrified! I was afraid I was going to lose you, and I didn't want to. You're a really special girl, Serena."

"I am?" I whispered, my heart pounding wildly.

"Incredibly special," Sonny murmured.

We looked at each other, and it was as if the world only existed for the two of us. I knew that something magical was about to happen.

It did. Sonny's lips came down gently on my own. It was a soft, warm kiss that only lasted seconds, but it was absolutely wonderful.

My romantic daydreams were all coming true!

Chapter Six

That night I went to bed early, but I couldn't fall asleep. Instead, I stared dreamily at my ceiling and thought about Sonny.

He had actually kissed me! Just remembering that miraculous moment made my lips tingle. Sonny really liked me! And he didn't even seem to notice the scars on my leg, or my limp. I was so glad he had a weakness for mermaids!

I felt incredibly happy—and incredibly confused. I cared about Sonny, and Sonny seemed to care about me. But right now he was at the Spring Fling with Diane.

Sure, Diane had said she wasn't romantically interested in Sonny, but how could she resist him? How could Sonny help being attracted to Diane? How could they go on a date and feel nothing for each other? They were such fun, special people, and I liked them so much.

I realized that I had made a stupid mistake by refusing to go to the dance. Both Diane and Sonny had begged me to go over and over again, but I'd said no. I should have said yes. So what if I couldn't dance? The dancing part wasn't important. What *was* important was being there with Sonny.

I glanced at my bedside clock and grimaced. Nine-thirty. Right about now Diane was probably in Sonny's arms. His cheek was resting against her silky brown hair, and his arms were holding her close. Diane's graceful, perfect legs were swaying and spinning in rhythm with Sonny's. And all eyes were undoubtedly on the striking couple.

"But they *aren't* a couple!" I said out loud. "Diane told me so. And Sonny called me special and he kissed me. That had to mean something!" But what?

Only the future would tell exactly what that *something* was.

* * *

Sunday came and went with no phone call from either Sonny or Diane. Not that I really expected either of them to call, but it would have been nice. So I was more than pleased to see Diane Monday morning in English.

"Hi, Diane," I said, slipping into my chair and turning around.

"Hi, yourself." Diane smiled. "Hey, I like your hair that way. You should wear it loose more often."

Self-consciously I reached up and pushed my hair away from my face. "I'm glad you like it. I got tired of that boring braid."

"I bet Sonny will approve, too. It makes you look more like a sea nymph. When we were dancing Saturday, Sonny kept talking about his 'special mermaid,' and how he tried to save you from a man-eating dolphin!" She giggled. "You may not have been at the dance in person, but you certainly were in spirit."

"Really?" I asked, delighted. "He really talked about me?"

"Only about every other sentence."

"Really?"

Diane rolled her eyes. "Yes, *really*. How many times do I have to say it? What am I? A messenger between you guys?"

I laughed. "It's just that I haven't heard from Sonny since Saturday afternoon. I've been wondering about . . . things."

Diane said, "Sonny was busy with his family all day Sunday, so I'm not surprised you didn't hear from him. Hey, what happened on that picnic anyway? Sonny wouldn't give me any details—he just said he had a good time. Exactly *how* good a time was it?"

I just shook my head. "No time for talking now—Mr. Swaine just walked in."

"We'll talk at lunch then."

"I'll be sitting under my usual tree."

"I know, but—" Diane hesitated. "Couldn't you eat inside for once? Join us in the cafeteria. I hate having to choose between you and Pam. We had a long talk yesterday and I'm afraid Pam resents my friendship with you."

That made me feel guilty. I liked Diane too much to cause her problems. It wouldn't kill me just this once to eat in the cafeteria, I decided, so I told Diane I'd meet her there.

After English, when I stopped by my locker, I was surprised to find Sonny waiting for me. He was holding his books in one hand and a wildflower in the other.

"Serena, I picked this especially for you. I

hope you like it," he said, handing me the flower.

I smiled radiantly at him. "It's lovely," I said. "Thanks."

"I've been thinking about you a lot since our picnic," he said.

"It was pretty special," I said softly.

"To me, too," Sonny replied, moving closer. "I hated going to the dance without you. Promise me you'll come to the next one. There's a major cotillion at the country club coming up in two weeks."

I was so excited that all I could do was nod. There was no way I could refuse him now, not even if I was on crutches!

He grinned. "Super! We'll have a fantastic time—you, me, and Diane."

"And Diane?"

"Sure," Sonny replied. "My dad's bank is sponsoring the cotillion and he expects me to take Diane. I can't suddenly dump her— it wouldn't be right. You understand, don't you?"

I frowned a little. "Yes, I guess I do," I said slowly, not quite sure if I was telling the truth.

"Great!" Sonny said, brushing his lips

against my forehead. "You're terrific, Serena. Lucky me, having you as my girl."

"Your girl?" I whispered, astonished. "As in *girlfriend*?"

He grinned. "If you'll have me."

"Oh, yes!" I murmured happily, hardly aware of all the kids rushing past us on their way to class.

The bell rang and Sonny said, "We'll talk more later." Then he hurried down the hall.

I looked down at the wildflower and smiled dreamily. Sonny wanted me to be his girl-friend! I could hardly believe it!

But then I remembered that Diane would be going to the dance with us, and I felt a pang of doubt. Was I really Sonny's girl, or just *one* of Sonny's girls? I couldn't help wondering if I would always have to share him with Diane. Was I becoming half of a *couple* or one-third of a *trio*?

"Over here, Serena," Diane called as I entered the cafeteria an hour later.

Catching sight of her and several other girls from the swim team, I walked over and took an empty chair next to Diane.

"You know the gang, Serena," Diane said

as I pulled a banana out of my lunch. "Andrea, Raelene, Tara, and Pamela."

Three of the four girls smiled and greeted me, but Pamela just nodded stiffly. Her hazel eyes were cool.

Diane told me that Sonny was busy arbitrating a case for student court and he wouldn't be at lunch today. "He'll pick us up after swim practice, though," Diane added.

"We were just talking about the Country Club Cotillion," Raelene said, pushing up her wire-framed glasses. "Are you going, Serena?"

"The cotillion?" I repeated. "Yes—yes, I'm going." Though I'd agreed to go to the dance, thinking about it made me uncomfortable. The fact remained, I didn't know how to dance.

"It'll be a major event," Diane said, smiling. "Ten times fancier than the Spring Fling. Sonny's father's bank is hosting it as a fundraiser for our swim team. I can't wait!"

"It's in two weeks, isn't it?" I asked, a memory clicking in my head. "Isn't that the same weekend as the regional swim meet?"

"Yeah. The cotillion will be kind of like a celebration dance. I'm excited just thinking about it!" Andrea said.

"It will only be a celebration *if* we win the meet," Tara added. "I sure hope we do."

"There'll be lots of society people there," Pamela commented airily. "Sonny's father is inviting all his business associates. Diane's mother has volunteered to chair the decoration committee, and my father's newspaper will provide the publicity." She turned to me. "What about you, Serena? Are your parents contributing anything to the cotillion?"

I looked down at the uneaten banana in my hand. "I don't have any parents. They died several years ago."

There was a brief silence, and then Diane said quickly, "But Serena has a terrific grandmother. You should see the weird hats she wears! I'll bet Lenora would help out. She's an artist."

"An artist?" Andrea asked. "Hey, that's cool."

"I'm sure Lenora would be happy to help with the decorations or something," I said, flashing Diane a grateful smile. "I'll ask her."

Tara grinned. "And with Serena on the team, we're sure to win the meet! I've never seen such strong strokes."

"Yeah, Serena, you're one radical swimmer. Have you ever considered going out for the Olympics?" Raelene asked.

I shrugged, unwilling to admit that before my accident, I had dreamed of doing just that.

"Really, Rae," Pamela said lightly, "what a silly question! Serena couldn't possibly compete in the Olympics. Who ever heard of a handicapped Olympic swimmer?"

"Pam!" Diane gasped. "How could you say such a mean thing?"

"I wasn't being mean—just truthful," Pamela said calmly. "Frankly, I'm getting a little tired of all this fuss over Serena. So, she's a good swimmer. Big deal. We're *all* good swimmers, or we wouldn't be on the team."

I could feel my cheeks reddening. I had known Pamela resented me, but until that moment I'd had no idea how much.

"It *is* a big deal," Diane defended me. "Serena's probably the best swimmer we've ever had."

"Better than me?" Pamela challenged, her hazel eyes narrowing. "Is that what you're saying?"

Diane shook her head. "No. You're putting words into my mouth. Like you said, we're all good swimmers."

"Sure," Pamela snapped, standing up. "I get the message loud and clear, Diane. Ever since Little Miss Mermaid here joined the team, you've turned your back on our friendship. What I don't get is *why*?"

"Pam, calm down," Diane said, putting a hand on Pamela's arm. "Nothing's changed with our friendship, and there's no reason for you to be nasty to Serena."

"I have plenty of reason," Pamela replied, giving me a fierce glance. "And so do you, Diane. Serena's no friend of yours. Just this morning I saw her snuggling up to Sonny— *your* boyfriend."

"I've told you a million times, Pam," Diane said with a sigh, "Sonny and I are just good friends. It's convenient for us to go places together sometimes, but he's *not* my boyfriend."

"I don't believe that for a minute," Pamela said sharply. "I've seen you in love too many times not to recognize when you're crazy about a guy."

Diane looked away. "You don't know what you're talking about, Pam."

"Don't I?" Pamela asked. "Didn't you go to the Spring Fling with Sonny?"

"Yes, but just as *friends*." Diane sighed again. "I really wish you'd stop trying to run my life, Pam. We're not little kids anymore."

Pamela flushed. I could tell Diane's words had hurt her, and I felt uncomfortable and even a little sorry for her.

"I can't believe what I'm hearing," Pamela said angrily. Then she faced me. "It's all your fault. You've turned my best friend against me! Well, I'm not about to stick around where I'm not wanted." And with that, she stomped away.

After she left, the conversation was stilted, and I felt guilty. I knew it was all my fault. I should have made more of an effort to make friends with Pamela for Diane's sake. Instead, I now had an enemy in Pamela Thorne.

And at the end of swimming practice, Pamela had an even stronger reason to dislike me. Barbara made the official announcement that I was replacing Pamela as lead swimmer.

Chapter Seven

"Where's Diane?" Sonny asked as I stepped out of the girls' locker room when practice was over.

"She's inside," I answered, weaving my long, damp hair into a braid as we walked down the hall. "Diane's going to ride home with Pamela today."

Sonny looked surprised. "She is? Why?"

"Because Pamela's upset, and she needs a friend right now." I hesitated, then added, "Our swim coach appointed a new lead swimmer."

"Too bad for Pam. Who's her replacement?" Sonny asked, walking with me down the steps and across the parking lot.

My cheeks grew warm. "Uh . . . me," I mumbled.

"Really?" Sonny grinned. "Wow! That's great!"

"Not as great as you'd think," I said, feeling guilty again. Pamela wasn't my favorite person in the world, but I had no desire to hurt her.

Sonny was still grinning. "Well, I can't say that I'm surprised." He reached for my hand and squeezed it. "Congratulations, Serena."

He took a bunch of keys out of his pocket and stopped in front of a beige Buick sedan.

"Is this your car?" I asked. I hadn't expected that Sonny would drive such a serious, sedate vehicle. "Somehow I expected a blazing-red sports car or something."

"Don't I wish!" Sonny said with a laugh. "Maybe in another life. For now, Dad lets me use this car."

"Oh, so it's your father's car," I said, getting in the passenger side and fastening my seat belt.

"One of his *old* cars," Sonny said, sitting next to me and fastening his seat belt, too. "Edward Alexander Sinclair the Third is

72

pretty status conscious—I haven't earned the right to drive the Mercedes yet. If you haven't guessed, he's not exactly an ordinary parent."

"So we have something in common," I joked. "My grandmother isn't ordinary, either."

Sonny turned the ignition key. "But my father and your grandmother are complete opposites. Dad's extremely ambitious and conservative. But your grandmother seems really easygoing. She lets you be yourself. I'm sure living with her is very interesting."

I laughed. "That's an understatement! Lenora's more than interesting. She's completely unpredictable and she's usually a lot of fun, but sometimes she can be exasperating. Still, you're right about her letting me be myself. She doesn't push me to do things her way. She's pretty cool."

"Speaking of cool, would you like me to turn up the air conditioner?" Sonny asked. "Are you comfortable?"

I smiled. Of course I was comfortable, not to mention thrilled, excited, and joyously content. For at least this short ride, Sonny and I were alone. No Diane—just us. For these few wonderful moments, I didn't have to share the boy I loved.

"I'm fine," I answered, glancing out the window to hide my reddening cheeks. Then we passed a street sign that I didn't recognize. "Only I'm not so sure about you. This isn't the way home. You must have made a wrong turn."

"No, I didn't." Sonny's smile was mysterious. "I know exactly where I'm going."

"What do you mean? Aren't you taking me home?"

"Eventually. But first I'm kidnapping you," Sonny said cheerfully.

I stared at him in astonishment. "You're *what*?"

"Kidnapping you. Do you mind?" Sonny asked.

"I guess not," I said with a little laugh. "So where are we going?"

Sonny slowed the car and made a sharp left turn into a big parking lot. I looked up and read flashing neon letters on a tall, square building: KNDE.

"What are we doing here? I thought you didn't work on Mondays," I said, unbuckling my seat belt.

Sonny walked around and held my door open for me. "You got it. That's why we're here. If I were working, I wouldn't be free to show my favorite girl around."

Favorite girl! I grinned happily at the phrase. Feeling as if I were floating instead of walking, I followed Sonny through the glass double doors.

We stopped briefly at the guard's desk and, while Sonny signed in, I called Lenora to let her know I'd be home late. Then Sonny and I went up an elevator and got off on the third floor.

"This is where I work," Sonny said, leading the way through a door with a gold embossed KNDE sign on it.

Immediately I had the sensation of entering a dazzling foreign world. The room hummed with activity: machines, voices, and strange bleeps and buzzes filled the room. A man was working at a computer console of some kind and a woman sat nearby with one ear pressed against a phone receiver. Other people were sitting at desks and shuffling papers. Off to my right was a soundproof area where a sign flashed ON THE AIR. Through a glass window I glimpsed a man and a woman wearing headphones and speaking into microphones.

"Awesome," I whispered to Sonny. "No wonder you love working here!"

Sonny beamed. "Come on—I'll introduce you to some of my friends."

The man at the computer console scratched his neatly trimmed beard and grinned. "Yo, Sonny. What are you wasting your time hanging around here for?"

"I'm a sucker for punishment, I guess," Sonny joked. "Jasper Bolton, meet Serena Waller."

I smiled and shyly said, "Hi."

Jasper gave a friendly salute. "Always glad to meet friends of Sonny's. Especially pretty girls." He gave Sonny a devilish wink.

Sonny slipped an arm around my shoulders and led me to an attractive olive-skinned woman with lively dark eyes. He introduced her as Juanita Rodriguez, the office manager, adding that she was like a second mother to him.

Next I met four people behind familiar voices—KNDE's nutty weatherman, Joker Jeff Kochman; financial reporter Dennis Hapka; and the jovial news team of Jean and Gene, one a round, bald man and the other a petite blond woman who looked about twenty-five.

KNDE was definitely a happening, spectacular place. How could Sonny even consider a dull future in finance after working here?

"Where are we going now?" I asked as he led me down a narrow hallway, then pushed open an unmarked door.

He flipped on a light. "This is a combination office and storeroom. Quiet and private. The perfect place for part two of my surprise."

"Part two?" I asked, grinning. "You mean there's more?"

Sonny nodded and pointed to a green cushioned chair. "You sit down while I put on a tape." He took a cassette out of his pocket and popped it into a small tape deck. Immediately the room filled with music—not hard rock, rap, or even rock and roll, but a soft, sweet, mellow tune. Sonny took my hand, and his gentle touch sent fiery tingles up my spine. "Come over here, Serena. Time for your first lesson."

"Lesson in what?"

"What else?" He laughed and put his arms around me. "Dancing. Just because you have a slight limp doesn't mean you can't learn to dance."

My eyes widened. "Are you serious?"

"Sure am."

"But I can't do it!" I cried, suddenly panic stricken.

"Maybe you can't break dance or pirouette like a ballerina, but there's no reason why you can't learn a simple slow dance. I figured if we practice together, we'll have a head start on the cotillion."

"I don't know about this. . . ." I murmured, but my body was already swaying to the music.

I rested my head against his shoulder and let Sonny lead me. The music seemed to relax my legs. Sensations of warmth and contentment enveloped me, and I found myself wondering whose rapid heartbeat I was hearing—Sonny's or mine?

"You're doing great," Sonny said, smiling down at me.

"This is kind of fun," I admitted, feeling breathless. "And I like this song."

"It's called 'Sweet Magic,'" Sonny said huskily. "From now on, whenever I hear it, I'll think of you."

"Our song," I said softly, then winced as my bad leg hit Sonny's knee.

"Put your foot against mine," Sonny said quickly. "Yeah, that's the idea. Just lean against me—you can do it," he whispered, lightly stroking my hair.

I did as he suggested, and suddenly I wasn't nervous anymore. "Wow, I'm really dancing," I whispered. "I—I can't believe it. I didn't think it was possible!"

"A lot of things are possible," he said, his blue eyes gazing tenderly into mine.

"Even us?" I asked breathlessly. I needed so badly to know exactly where I stood with him.

He said, "I care about you, Serena. You have to know that by now."

"I think I do, but . . ."

"But what?" he asked.

I swallowed hard. "I'm just a little confused about . . . about going to the cotillion."

"Hey, Twinkle-Toes," Sonny teased, "You're now a dynamite slow dancer. What's to worry about?"

"It's not the dancing. . . ." I took a deep breath, and for a moment I stood still. "It's you, me, and"—I hesitated—"and Diane."

"What about Diane?" Sonny asked.

"I just feel funny about triple dating, I guess," I confessed.

"Oh," Sonny said, frowning. "I thought I explained about that. With Dad's bank sponsoring the cotillion, I'm kind of a cohost, and Dad assumes Diane will be a hostess."

"So where does that leave me?" I asked softly.

"Dancing in my arms all night," Sonny said, tightening his arms around me. "Really, it'll be fine. After all the official stuff, it'll be just you and me. There'll be plenty of guys for Diane to dance with."

"I suppose so," I said without conviction.

Sonny gazed thoughtfully into my eyes. "I guess I'm not being fair to you, am I? I know I wouldn't like it if I had to share you with another guy. Would it make you feel better if I talked to Diane? I could see if she can find someone else to take her to the cotillion."

I wanted to be with Sonny, but not at Diane's expense. "No—no, don't," I said quickly. "But maybe you could tell your father about us. Couldn't you tell him I'm your real date?"

"Well, I guess so. Sure, why not?" Sonny replied. "Then you and Diane could both be hostesses." His tone sounded light, but his eyes looked worried. "Dad will just have to understand that I'm old enough to make some of my own decisions—like who I date. I'll talk to him tonight."

"Good. Then everything will be perfect," I

murmured as we resumed my dancing lesson. It was nice being in Sonny's arms, but somehow the mood had changed.

A little voice in my head kept asking why Sonny seemed uneasy about talking about me to his father. The voice taunted, *Maybe he's ashamed of you.*

But I told the voice to shut up.

Chapter Eight

Several days later Diane and I were lounging in my bedroom. I was draped across my bed on my stomach and Diane sat at my desk, a pencil in her hand and a piece of paper in front of her.

"Earth to Serena," Diane teased. "Are you ready to come down for a landing yet? I really need some help designing an ad for the cotillion."

"I'm sorry, Diane," I said. "I guess I was daydreaming again."

"Again?" Diane laughed. "More like *still*. And I can just bet I know who you're day-dreaming about."

My cheeks grew warm. "Am I *that* obvious?"

"Well, it's obvious to me. You're easier to read than a picture book."

"I guess I have been a bit preoccupied," I admitted. I knew I was definitely in love. On the drive home from the radio station on Monday, Sonny and I had talked about every topic under the sun. I was thrilled to discover how easy it was to confide in him. And if Monday was wonderful, Tuesday, Wednesday, and Thursday were even better, because they began a routine I hoped would last forever. Sonny and I managed to see each other at least three times each day—five minutes of small talk before school, at lunch underneath a willow tree, and a quick kiss before I hurried to swimming practice. I felt like a different girl from the one who had considered herself a loner with no friends and no prospect of romance.

"Snap out of it, Serena," Diane ordered, clapping her hands loudly. "I need some input on this ad. If I can deliver it to Sonny's father today, he said the bank's public relations person would include it in the newsletter they give out to their customers. But I can't think of anything to write."

"Don't look at me. I know zilch about stuff like that," I replied.

Diane sighed. "Me, too. That's why I'm having so much trouble. Don't you have *any* ideas?"

"Not really," I told her. "Lenora's the artistic one in this family, not me. All I know about is sea life. Ask me something easy—about jellyfish, algae, or dolphins. Oh, and speaking of dolphins, guess what I saw this morning?"

"Your dolphin friend?"

"Yes, but more!" I exclaimed. "Twinkie has a family now! I saw him swimming with a mother dolphin and her baby."

"That sounds neat," Diane said. "I'd love to see them sometime."

"How about now?" I suggested. "I'm tired of being cooped up in the house. We could go to the beach."

Diane shook her head. "No way! I have to do this ad, remember? And you're supposed to be helping me."

"I guess I'm having trouble concentrating today."

"And I know why!" Diane wagged a finger at me. "You have a major case of Sonny Sinclairitis."

I giggled. "An astute diagnosis, Dr. Diane. Is my condition serious?"

"Very serious," Diane said solemnly. "I'm afraid there is absolutely no cure."

"I sure hope not," I said. "You know, feeling this way is super and yet so weird. It's been years since I liked a boy. Three years to be exact."

"Anybody I know?"

"No. That was before I moved here," I answered. I didn't want to mention that Jon had dumped me shortly after the car accident. "Anyway, Sonny's a hundred times more wonderful than Jon. I feel pretty lucky."

"You and Sonny are both lucky. I'm really happy for you."

"You don't know how glad I am to hear you say that," I said sincerely, walking over and looking at Diane's paper. So far the only penciled words were COUNTRY CLUB COTILLION.

"Being in love has to be the most thrilling thing in the world," Diane said, sounding oddly wistful. "Especially when both people are so well suited. I really envy you."

"*You* envy *me*?" I asked in surprise. "That's hard to believe. You're so—so perfect."

"Watch out for people who seem to be perfect," Diane stated. "Nine times out of ten they're just trying to cover up their insecurities."

I gave her a sharp look. "Is something bothering you, Diane?"

She shrugged. "Not really. Just a silly daydream—a wish for something that could never, ever come true."

"Please tell me about it," I urged.

"It's nothing, really," Diane said sadly. "Just a boy I kind of like, but he'd never go for me."

"You're underestimating yourself, Diane. You could have your pick of any of the guys at school," I told her.

She shook her head. "Not this one."

"Tell me more—like who this guy is," I said. My heart was pounding as I waited for Diane's answer. She had said she wasn't interested in Sonny, but maybe she meant *he* wasn't interested in *her*. Silently I prayed, *Please don't let her say it's Sonny.*

"I don't know if I should," Diane mumbled. "When I told Pam, she laughed at me."

I reached out and touched her hand. "I would never laugh at you, Diane. You can confide in me and I won't tell anybody, I promise."

Diane stared intently into my face. Slowly

her frown changed to a half smile. "Well, the boy I like is really smart, cute, and terribly interesting."

That fits Sonny, I thought, feeling uneasy.

"And his name . . ." I held my breath. "His name is . . . Melvin Engeldinger."

My mouth dropped open. *Melvin?* Smart? Yes. Interesting? I suppose. But cute? No way! Melvin's teeth filled up half his face and his eyes were a little too close together for my taste. The word *nerd* was written all over him—and yet Diane actually liked him! Love was definitely strange!

"Well?" Diane asked me eagerly. "What do you think?"

I was saved from answering, because just then there was a brisk tap on my door.

"Hello, girls," Lenora called, peeking into my room. "How are things going?"

"Just fine, Lenora," I said. "What's up?"

Lenora adjusted her black-net and ebony-pearled hat, and then came in. "I know you're working on that ad for the cotillion, and I thought I'd see if I could offer my assistance. Anything I can do?"

Diane pointed to the piece of paper on the desk. "I sure hope so! I promised Mr. Sinclair

I'd give it to him by tonight and I've barely started it."

"I'm well-versed in the art of publicity. I've done many an ad in my time," Lenora said, to my surprise. But then, Lenora was always full of surprises.

Diane's face brightened. "You have? I don't want to impose, but would you—I mean, would you mind . . . ?"

"I'd love to. It'll be fun," Lenora said, taking the paper from Diane. "Just fill me in on the details, and I'll come up with something spectacular. Perhaps boldfaced type with a silhouetted border of graceful girl swimmers. . . ."

"That sounds great!" Diane exclaimed.

"I'll start on it right now. It won't take long at all—perhaps a couple of hours. Is that soon enough?"

Diane gave a relieved sigh. "Fantastic! Wow, you're a real lifesaver. Thanks so much, Mrs. . . ." Diane hesitated and looked quizzically at my grandmother. "Mrs. what? I'm sorry, I don't remember Serena telling me your last name."

Lenora lifted her chin regally and smiled. "And you certainly won't hear it from *me*."

"Huh?" Diane asked, surprised.

"Titles such as Mrs. or Ms. are for *old* people. In the universal scheme of life, my spirit is young and continually evolving. My body may age, but never my soul. Jut call me Lenora." And with that, my grandmother nodded a good-bye to us and swept out of the room.

Diane and I stared at each other.

For a moment, we didn't say anything. Then we promptly burst into giggles.

Two hours later Diane pressed the doorbell of the Sinclairs' house, and I tried to stand up straight despite my trembling legs. For once this awkwardness had nothing to do with my injury. It was my body's response to fear, fear of meeting my boyfriend's parents for the first time. If only Sonny were home!

"Do you think Sonny will be back from the station yet?" I asked Diane nervously.

Diane shook her head. "No. His car wasn't in the driveway." She grinned at me. "Cheer up. You'll have plenty of chances to spend time with him. I can't wait to show his dad the ad, though. Lenora did a fantastic job.

Mr. Sinclair will definitely run it in the newsletter."

I smiled. "That would be great. Then tons of people will come to the cotillion."

I stiffened as I heard heavy footsteps approaching the door. Diane must have noticed my tension, because she whispered, "Relax. You'll love Sonny's father. He's really nice."

The door opened. A tall, blue-eyed man stood there. If his hair were thicker and a few shades lighter, it would be exactly like Sonny's.

"Why hello, Diane," Mr. Sinclair said warmly. "Come on in. Don't tell me you've already finished the cotillion ad."

"I promised it to you by tonight and here it is," Diane said, handing him the paper as we stepped inside.

Mr. Sinclair whistled. "Well, well! This is very impressive. Quite an improvement over last year's ad. I hadn't realized art was one of your many talents."

Diane beamed, then gestured at me. "I'm glad you like it, but I didn't do it. All the credit goes to Serena's grandmother."

Shyness filled me as I smiled tentatively at the father of the boy I loved. Several days ago

Sonny had said he'd tell his family about me. I wondered if he had, and if so, what he had said.

"Well, Serena, you obviously have a very talented grandmother." Mr. Sinclair tilted his head and rubbed his chin thoughtfully. "Hmm. Serena. . . . That name sounds familiar. I've heard that name before."

Any minute now Mr. Sinclair would realize I was the new girl in Sonny's life. I felt relieved and pleased. There would be no more confusion about who Sonny was actually dating, and his family would accept me as his girlfriend. I'd be a regular guest at the Sinclairs'.

Mr. Sinclair suddenly snapped his fingers. "I remember now," he exclaimed. "You're the new swimmer on the Farringdon girls' team. You took Pammy's lead position, right?"

Diane gave me an uneasy glance. "He means Pamela."

Mr. Sinclair grinned. "Yes, Pammy Thorne. A really sweet girl. Her father's one of my closest friends. I was sorry to hear about her being replaced, but I suppose Barbara knew what she was doing." He surveyed me with a critical squint. "You're undoubtedly a superb swimmer, or she wouldn't have given you Pammy's spot."

"Serena is like a fish in the water," Diane said proudly. "She's amazing."

I fidgeted nervously. It sounded as though Sonny's father knew nothing about me except what he had heard from Pamela's father.

"I suppose I'm a good swimmer," I said weakly. "But so are Diane and Pamela."

"I won't argue with you there," Mr. Sinclair said with a hearty chuckle. "After watching Diane and Pammy grow up, I know firsthand how good they are at everything they do. Especially little Di here," he added, laying a fond hand on Diane's shoulder.

"Please don't call me that," Diane protested. "Really, Mr. Sinclair, I'm not a little girl anymore."

"I can see that," Mr. Sinclair replied. "Sweet sixteen, aren't you?"

Diane blushed and nodded. "Four months younger than Sonny."

Mr. Sinclair grinned. "And you're both quite mature for your age—much like Emmy and I were when we were teenagers. When we turned eighteen, we formally announced our engagement. Not that I'm advocating young marriage, but I have nothing against long engagements," he added, giving Diane a meaningful wink.

"Mr. Sinclair!" Diane cried. "You don't know what you're talking about!"

"I can hope, can't I? As you know, I have very high hopes for you and my son."

I could feel the color draining out of my face. I couldn't believe what I was hearing. I didn't *want* to believe it.

Diane reached for my hand. "Serena, we'd better go now."

"So soon?" Mr. Sinclair asked. "Why not stay for dinner with us, Diane? Emmy was saying just this morning that you hadn't been around for a while. We'd really love to have you."

"No, thank you," Diane said quickly, flashing me a worried look. "Serena and I really have to leave."

Mr. Sinclair raised his eyebrows. "Of course, your friend is invited, too, Diane. It was rude of me not to make that clear."

Diane's friend. That was how Sonny's father regarded me? He didn't realize I was dating his son! Hadn't Sonny told him anything about me at all?

The answer was painfully obvious. Sonny's

father had no idea I even knew his son. Sonny hadn't told his father—or probably his mother, either—about me.

And there was only one reason I could think of as an explanation. I glanced down at my right leg. Sonny was ashamed of me.

Chapter Nine

That night, for the first time in two years, I dreamed about the accident.

My parents were taking me to a movie. I could hear their voices in the front seat of the car as I sat in the backseat, reading a book—it was a biography of Gertrude Ederle, a famous woman swimmer.

I was imagining how it would feel to be awarded an Olympic gold medal, when suddenly a loud screech, a crash, and then screams echoed around me. Another car had smashed into ours. I was engulfed in terror and unbearable pain.

And then my dream changed. I was lying

in a hospital bed with my leg elevated in a cast. Bandages were all over my body and my eyes stung from endless crying. The hospital door opened and a blond boy walked into the room—Jon. He had flowers in one hand and a wrapped package in the other, but the expression on his face was one of pity and dismay. As I watched, Jon's hair color seemed to darken and his features changed. It was no longer Jon standing there—it was Sonny.

"I can't be your boyfriend," he said, dropping the flowers and package on the floor. "You're not perfect. I'd be embarrassed to be seen with you."

"But I can't help it!" I could hear myself shouting. "The accident wasn't my fault!"

"My father wouldn't approve," he said. "You're not good enough for me. Not good enough . . . not good enough . . ."

"No, no!" I sobbed, my entire body trembling. Suddenly my eyes opened and I sat bolt upright in bed.

Drawing my knees up and wrapping my arms around them, I gasped for breath. My mind gradually cleared and I realized I was in my own bedroom, not a hospital room, and I was completely alone.

"Just a dream," I told myself, lying back

down and snuggling underneath the covers. "It was just a bad dream."

But as I tried to go back to sleep, a disturbing thought nagged at me. Maybe it had been more than a dream from the past. Maybe it was a premonition of the future. Was my heart going to be broken again, not by a blond boy named Jon this time, but by a brown-haired boy named Sonny?

"Are you sure you don't feel well enough to go to school?" Lenora asked with concern the following morning.

I leaned my head against a couch pillow and pulled an afghan over my body. "My head hurts and I'm exhausted—I think I might be coming down with something," I groaned. I had hardly slept a wink all night.

Taking a sip of coffee, Lenora leaned forward in her chair and regarded me closely. "You *do* look ill . . . but I get the feeling there's more to it than that. Do you have a difficult test today?"

I managed a small cough. "No. No tests. I just don't feel good."

"It's probably those early-morning swims of yours. The ocean is much too cold. No wonder you're sick!"

"That must be it," I said in a weak voice. I knew I was exaggerating my symptoms, and that my discomfort was more mental than physical, but I needed time to think about my relationship with Sonny. Since our first meeting everything had been happening so fast. All of a sudden my life had changed to include a friendship with Diane, the lead position on the school swim team, and a growing romance with Sonny—or at least that was what I had thought it was. While I figured things out, I just wanted to hide from the world.

Lenora gave me a few more curious glances, but soon she put on a ridiculous purple-suede hat and left the house for her boutique.

I buried my head in the couch pillow and promptly fell asleep.

Some time later I awoke to the phone's ringing.

Reaching for the living room entension, I mumbled, "Hello?"

"Serena, is that you?" a boy's voice asked.

"Yes . . . Sonny?"

"Over the phone lines and in person," Sonny said in his best "radio" voice. "Hey, how are you doing? I heard you were sick today. Hope it's nothing serious."

"Oh, it isn't. I'm feeling better already," I said, not quite truthfully. "Where are you calling from?"

"The school pay phone. It's lunch break, and I'm feeling awfully lonely here without you."

A hesitant smile touched my lips. Sonny always knew the perfect thing to say. No wonder I was crazy about him. But then I remembered my visit to his house yesterday, and my smile faded.

"Sonny, did you know I met your father yesterday?" I asked bluntly.

There was a brief pause. "Yeah, Dad mentioned it."

"Did he say anything about me?"

"He said you seemed very nice and kind of quiet. He also liked Lenora's work on the cotillion ad."

I clutched the receiver more tightly. "I'm glad. But I'm more interested in how he felt when you told him you were dating me. Was he disappointed to find out Diane isn't your girlfriend?"

Another pause. "Uh—no, he wasn't disappointed."

"What a relief!" I said. My spirits were improving rapidly. "What did you say when you asked about my being a hostess at the cotillion?"

"Uh . . . nothing," Sonny replied, evasively. "I—I didn't get around to asking him."

"You didn't?" I frowned. "Sonny, what exactly did you tell your parents about me?"

"Well, to be truthful, not a whole lot. You have to realize that talking to my dad isn't easy. He gets these stubborn ideas in his head. I mean . . ." Sonny's voice trailed off. Then he mumbled, "Dad doesn't know you're my girlfriend."

"You haven't told him?" I cried, all my insecurities rushing back.

"I wanted to, but there never seemed a right time," Sonny confessed. "But I'll tell him tonight, I promise."

Anger and hurt surged through me, but I kept my voice calm. "Your father thinks you're dating Diane, doesn't he?"

"Well . . . yeah." Sonny added quickly, "Look, the bell just rang and I've got to go. We'll have to finish this talk later. Can I come over after school?"

"Don't bother," I snapped. I couldn't pretend to be calm any longer. "Everything's suddenly very obvious to me." My dream flashed in my head. "I'm an embarrassment

102

to you. You're ashamed to tell your folks about me. And I know why—it's because of my leg."

"*What?* Serena, you're talking crazy!"

"So now I'm crazy, too!" I yelled. "Well, you don't have to talk to this crazy, limping freak ever again! Good-bye, Sonny Sinclair!"

And then I slammed the receiver down.

I sobbed and moped around all day until Diane called later that afternoon.

"How are you feeling?" she asked.

"Not too great," I said, rubbing my swollen eyes. "Aren't you still at school?"

"Yeah, but I managed to get out of sixth period early so I could call you."

"You sound strange—is something up?" I asked.

"You guessed it. And if you aren't too terribly sick, you really should come to practice," Diane said urgently. "Barbara's called a special meeting to talk about the regional meet. If you don't show up, she may reinstate Pam as lead swimmer."

"Why would she do that? Just tell Barbara I'm sick."

"I don't know if that will be good enough," Diane said. She sounded really worried. "Pam told me that your being absent is the best thing that could happen to her. So unless you're violently ill, you'd better come."

I wasn't sure what to say. Any sickness I felt was in my heart, not in the rest of me. Physically I was up to swimming, if not emotionally.

"I don't have a way to get to school," I said, latching onto a convenient excuse.

"Easily solved. I can be there in eight minutes," Diane said, mistaking my meaning. "Bye!" The phone went dead before I could make up any more excuses.

Twenty minutes later I was doing warm-up exercises with the other swim-team members. Being out in the fresh air and stretching my muscles was invigorating. Some of the tension eased out of my body, and I truly enjoyed seeing Pamela's annoyance at the sight of me.

"I thought you were supposed to be sick," she said in an accusing tone.

"I'm a quick healer," I replied coolly, and dove into the pool.

Swimming practice was more strenuous than usual because Barbara wanted us to be ready for the upcoming meet. By banishing all thoughts of Sonny to a dark corner of my mind I was able to concentrate on swimming and nothing else.

Afterward, Barbara called us together for a strategy meeting. She praised our good points and suggested areas for individual improvement. She told me that I was doing okay on all but the breaststroke, and I promised to put in extra practice hours to strengthen it. Barbara ended the discussion with a pep talk, reminding all of us that our team had a good chance at being number one—an honor we all wanted to achieve.

"Great workout," Diane said, falling in step beside me after Barbara had dismissed us. "I'm all hyped about this meet. It'll be great."

I nodded. "I'm looking forward to it, too." And I was. It was *all* I had to look forward to now.

We walked into the locker room. As we started for the showers, I remembered that I had left my cap outside.

"Oops, I forgot my cap. I'll be back in a minute," I told Diane, and hurried back to the pool.

Two people were still hanging out there— Pamela and Raelene. *Darn!* The last thing I needed right now was a confrontation with

Pamela. I decided to come back after I had showered and changed.

As I was returning to the locker room I heard my name mentioned. Staying in the shadow of a wall, I moved closer to Pamela and Raelene.

"Who does she think she is, anyway?" Pamela was saying irritably.

"Serena's not so bad," Raelene replied. *Thanks for the wholehearted endorsement, Rae,* I thought.

"Maybe not, but she's not so good, either. If I hear another person say how great a swimmer she is, I swear I'm going to puke!"

"Well, with her on the team we have a good shot at the regionals," Raelene said.

"I know that—boy, do I know that," Pamela said, sounding exasperated. "It's the only thing keeping me from telling her off to her face. I'll never forgive her for turning Diane against me and stealing my position on the team."

"Don't let her get to you, Pam. Everybody on the team likes you better than her anyway."

I gasped in shock. I had thought Rae was my friend!

"I know, and I keep reminding myself she's our ticket to a first-place trophy."

"You got it. So we'll just have to be nice to her until swimming season is over."

Pamela sighed. "That long? I guess I can survive, but I get so angry sometimes. And you know what else really steams me?"

"What?"

"The way Serena's always making sappy eyes at Sonny. As though a guy like Sonny could actually be interested in a girl like her."

A wave of nausea rushed through me. Pamela had just voiced my deepest secret fear.

Raelene said, "But Sonny seems to like her, too. Why would he pretend?"

Pamela laughed. "Who knows? Maybe he feels sorry for her. It's a good thing she knows how to swim, because she certainly can't *walk* like a normal person."

Tears filled my eyes, and I stumbled away. I couldn't stand to listen anymore. I felt humiliated, ashamed, and more alone than I had ever been in my life. What hurt the most was realizing that Raelene, who I had thought was my friend, wasn't really my friend, after all. She had only been pretending.

Could I trust anybody? What about the other girls on the swim team, Diane, and even Sonny?

Chapter Ten

On the drive home from practice I was silent. Pamela and Raelene's cruel words kept ringing in my head. I felt like such a fool. Was everyone on the team laughing at me behind my back?

"Is something wrong, Serena?" Diane asked at last.

I shook my head, keeping my face averted to hide my moist eyes.

"Are you sure?" she persisted. "You've been acting weird ever since we got in the car."

"It's nothing. I'm just a little tired."

"I hope you're not sick, like you were earlier today. I'd feel terrible if you got pneumonia or something because I forced you to come to practice. Maybe I should have let you stay home and rest."

"Maybe you should have," I mumbled.

Out of the corner of my eye, I saw Diane give me a puzzled look. "Are you mad at me for something, Serena?"

"Of course not."

"Then why won't you look at me? Did I do or say something that's upset you?"

"No—not you." The passing scenery blurred in my vision as tears slid down my cheeks.

"Then who?" Diane said angrily. "Not Pam again?"

I didn't say anything.

"Pam said something nasty when you went to get your swim cap, didn't she? I wondered why you came back without it. So what did she say? She isn't still insisting that Sonny is my boyfriend, is she? Because you know he isn't. Sonny's nuts about you."

I lifted my head and this time I met Diane's questioning eyes. "If he's so nuts about me, why is he keeping me a big secret from his parents? His father practically has the two of you married!"

"I know that, but that's ridiculous. I only

like Sonny as a friend. Melvin's the one I really care about—I told you that."

"Then why haven't you told *Melvin*?" I asked. "Why don't you admit your feelings to him? Better yet, ask him to be your date for the cotillion."

Diane gave a little gasp, her knuckles whitening as she gripped the steering wheel. "You can't be serious! He doesn't know I'm alive. What if he laughs at me?"

"Then at least you'll know where you stand," I said wearily. "And that's more than I know about me and Sonny." I sighed deeply. "My life might have been kind of dull, but it sure wasn't this complicated before I met Sonny and joined the swim team. Now I don't know who to believe about anything."

"You can believe me," Diane said softly.

"I know," I said, but felt uneasy as I remembered Pamela's words. I was fairly sure Diane genuinely liked me, but now I knew that both Pamela and Raelene didn't. What about the other girls on the team? Were any of them real friends?

And as for Sonny—well, I was beginning to wish I'd never met Sonny Sinclair. As it was, Sonny and I were through. After our argument on the phone today, I was sure he must hate me. I'd told him never to speak to me again, and he probably wouldn't. Soon he'd start dating a new girl—someone perfect like Diane, who he'd be proud to introduce to his parents.

"Twinkie!" I called, walking along the surf a while later. "Are you out there somewhere?"

I shaded my eyes with one hand and peered across the ocean. I saw sparkling waves and a few sea gulls screeching overhead, but there was no sign of my dolphin friend.

"Twinkie—hey boy, where are you?" I called again.

"Darn," I muttered to myself. I'd really hoped to talk to him today. After Mr. Sinclair yesterday and Pamela today, I was sure that telling my troubles to Twinkie would help.

Feeling miserable and lonely, I sank down onto the beach. I dipped my index finger into the sand, and traced the word *Sonny*. Underneath it I wrote my own name. And then I swept both names away.

Sonny's face materialized in my mind and I felt my heart wrench unbearably. I loved him so much! I wondered how long it would take me to forget him. Weeks? Months? Years? Or maybe never?

I felt an urge to run into the house and call him, but I resisted. A phone call wouldn't change anything. I'd still be an embarrassment to him. If only things could have been different. . . .

A shrill sound broke into my thoughts and I looked up to see Twinkie dancing on his tail out in the ocean.

"Hi, fella!" I cried, standing up. "It's about time you showed up."

Twinkie leaped into the air, then dove underneath the water. When he resurfaced, he made a loud clacking noise.

"Want to play?" I called.

The dolphin made a louder noise and then dove again. Reappearing, he slapped his round nose against the waves and made a high-pitched, demanding sound. I'd never seen him act that way before. Was something wrong?

"Twinkie, what is it?" I asked, wading into the surf until the waves splashed the hem of my shorts.

The dolphin jumped and squawked some more, almost as if he wanted me to follow him.

"Okay," I yelled. "I'll come just as soon as I change into my swimsuit. I promise I'll be back in a minute."

I turned and ran up the beach path to my house. I couldn't for the life of me guess what was going on with Twinkie, but I planned to find out.

By the time I flung open my front door I was panting. I paused to catch my breath, and then went inside. If I was lucky, Lenora would still be at her shop. I knew my grandmother wouldn't appreciate my going into the ocean on the very day I had been too "sick" to go to school.

Tiptoeing down the hall, I gasped when I saw not Lenora, but Diane.

"What are you doing here?" I exclaimed.

"Waiting for you," Diane replied, smiling. "The door was unlocked, so I came right in."

"But it's only been an hour since you dropped me off."

"I know." Her smile widened. "Just enough time to solve the problems of the world. *My* world, anyway!"

"What are you talking about?" I asked. "No, wait—don't tell me. Tell me while we go down to the beach. First I have to get into my swimsuit," I added, motioning for Diane to follow me to my room.

"You're going swimming? Haven't you had enough water for one day?"

I put my finger to my lips. "Keep it down. If Lenora's anywhere around, I'd rather she didn't find out—not yet, anyway."

"Why all the mystery?" Diane asked.

"Twinkie's freaking out," I said, slipping into a one-piece suit. "I think he wants to show me something."

"What?"

"How should I know?" I asked, slinging a towel over my shoulder as we left my bedroom. "But he's really upset. I've never seen him act like this before."

I opened the back door and we stepped outside.

"Now we can talk freely," I said, walking faster than Diane, despite my problem leg. Apparently, when my mind was occupied with something other than myself, my limp wasn't as pronounced. Could my deformity be more in my mind than in my body? I wondered. I'd have to think about that later. "So, what did you want to tell me, Diane?"

Diane answered. "I just wanted to say thank you, I'm sorry, and you're the best friend in the entire world!"

"Huh? Run that by me again," I said, pausing to stare at her.

"Well, after our talk earlier I felt really guilty."

"About what?" I asked, starting to jog.

"About you and Sonny," she told me. "The minute I knew you were interested in him, I should have said I wouldn't go out with him again. It wasn't fair of me to expect you to share your boyfriend."

"He's not my boyfriend . . . not anymore," I said sadly. "We just had a big fight."

"Then you have to make up! I want you to be as happy as I am—especially since my happiness is all due to you!"

"Me? What did I do?"

"You told me to be honest about my feelings for Melvin. So I took your advice." She giggled. "I asked him to be my date for the cotillion, and he accepted. I can't believe how easy it was!"

I flashed Diane a sincere smile, happy that she had a boy who really cared about her. "I'm glad things are working out for you."

"And they can work out for you, too,"

Diane said, increasing her pace to keep up with me.

"Only if a miracle happens," I said wryly. "But I don't want to talk about my problems. Right now I'm more concerned about Twinkie."

"What do you think is the matter with him?"

"I wish I knew. Yesterday when I saw him he was swimming with his new lady friend and her baby— Maybe something's happened to them! Maybe that's why he was acting so frantic." I grabbed Diane's hand. "Come on— we have to hurry!"

Minutes later, Diane watched from the shore as I dove into the water. Twinkie jumped and splashed excitedly, then headed north. I followed, my strokes smooth and swift. I was certain now that Twinkie's friends were in trouble. I only hoped I could do something to help.

I swam around a rocky area into the cove. At first I didn't see anything unusual. Then I looked at the shoreline, and my heart nearly stopped. A large gray shape was beached in the shallow surf. It was Twinkie's lady friend, and as I swam closer I realized with horror that she was ensnared in a large net! Floundering just a few feet away was the baby dolphin.

A sensation of panic filled me. What was I going to do? Even if I succeeded in freeing the mother dolphin from the net, I didn't have the strength to push her back into the ocean. The tide was inching lower and lower, and both mother and baby would surely die unless I got help from someone stronger than Diane.

A vision of a blue-eyed boy flickered in my mind. I was pretty sure Sonny would want to help, but did I have the courage to ask him?

Not really, but I'd do it anyway for the dolphins—and maybe even for me.

Chapter Eleven

Lenora had returned by the time I dashed wildly into the house. To say she was surprised to see me with dripping-wet hair and wearing a damp swimsuit would be an understatement. Four precious minutes were wasted as I proceeded to explain the dolphin dilemma to her.

Then I sprinted to the phone and quickly dialed Sonny's number. The phone rang twice, and then on the third ring he answered.

Nervousness and shyness momentarily took my breath away. Then I managed a feeble, "Uh—Sonny . . . it's me."

"Serena!" Sonny exclaimed. "I'm so glad

you called! I wanted to call you, but I didn't because I was afraid you'd hang up on me. I really feel crummy about—"

"There's no time for that now," I said, struggling to keep my emotions separate from my practical self. "Something terrible's happened! There's a dolphin trapped in a net and beached in the cove!"

I heard Sonny gasp, then he asked, "Is it Twinkie?"

"No, not him—his lady friend. At least I *think* she's his lady friend, but I don't know for sure," I babbled. "All I really know is that she may die if I can't free her. You'll help, won't you?"

"Absolutely," Sonny answered promptly. "I'll be there in fifteen minutes."

I sighed with relief and returned the receiver to its cradle.

Exactly twelve minutes later Sonny's car was pulling into my driveway. As he got out, his eyes met mine in an electric gaze filled with uncertainty and caring. I tingled all over, then mentally reprimanded myself for letting my emotions get the better of me when a dolphin's life was at stake. Right now, the dolphin was more important.

"Diane's waiting for us on the beach," I

said, leading the way. "We'll either have to swim to the cove or hike down the cliff."

"I'd rather hike," Sonny said. "It's not as treacherous a climb as it looks. I can go ahead and trample some of the thorny weeds to make it easier for you and Diane."

"You and Diane can go by land, but I'd rather go by sea. It's quicker and easier for me. You guys go ahead—I'll meet you at the cove."

Shortly afterward I was kneeling in the receding surf next to the female dolphin. She was resting in only a few inches of water, and the tide was ebbing lower and lower. There wouldn't be another high tide until late tonight, and I was worried that might be too late.

Patting the creature gently on her nose, I whispered, "Hang on, girl. We'll do what we can to save you."

Looking up, I saw Sonny and Diane inching down the hill. Sonny was in the lead, breaking the weedy trail with a large stick.

"How is she?" he asked, running over to kneel next to me.

"Not good," I replied grimly. "She's hardly moving at all."

"No big surprise," Sonny said, grimacing

at the net wrapped around the dolphin. "Let's see if this helps."

He reached into his pocket and pulled out a Swiss Army knife. He snapped it open and carefully began to cut away the net. Then he put away his knife and tenderly stroked the dolphin. Giving her a firm but gentle push, he said, "You're free now, girl. Go to your baby. Come on, girl, *move!*"

But the dolphin only made a mournful whining noise. She was obviously too weak to maneuver in only a puddle of water.

Sonny surveyed the dolphin, his expression serious. "She's in worse shape than I expected. We're going to need more help. Three people aren't enough to move her."

"We can try," Diane said. She bent over and reached for the dolphin's fluked tail, but her fingers slipped, and she stumbled backward.

"Give it up, Diane," Sonny said. "A full-grown dolphin weighs hundreds of pounds. We may need as many as a dozen people to budge her."

The enormity of the situation sank in. "What are we going to do?" I asked.

Sonny stood up. "Let's go up to your house and phone for help."

"Phone who?"

Sonny shrugged "The fire department, the police, the coast guard—I don't really know. Maybe we'll have to phone *all* of them!"

The Sea Mist Police Department told us to call the fire department, the fire department told us to call Animal Control, and Animal Control didn't answer. Then Diane found an emergency number for Animal Control, which I quickly dialed.

A gruff-sounding man answered, and when I filled him in on the situation he cleared his throat a few times, then said dolphins weren't his business.

"Why don't you call the police?" he suggested.

"I already have. And the fire department," I told him. "I don't know who else to try!"

"Well, don't bother with government or state offices, because nothing's going to be open on a Friday night. Anyone with any sense has gone home for the weekend." The man chuckled. "Hey, let me give you a piece of free advice. Just forget about the dolphin. So a dolphin dies—tuna boats slaughter hundreds of 'em all the time. What's one more fish, anyway?"

"For your information," I said furiously, "dolphins are mammals, like people. And maybe I can't save hundreds of dolphins from tuna fishermen, but I can try to save the one beached here!" I slammed the receiver down.

Lenora applauded, and Sonny reached out and squeezed my hand. "Way to go, Serena!"

Diane said, "Yeah, but now what do we do?"

"How about a veterinarian?" Lenora suggested.

"Good idea," Sonny said. "We might as well give it a try."

But that idea didn't work out, either. The first vet we called said he didn't treat dolphins, and a dolphin usually beaches itself when it is sick. I tried to explain that this dolphin had been caught in a net, but he said it didn't matter—as far as he was concerned, a beached dolphin would soon be a dead dolphin.

There was only one other vet in Sea Mist, Dr. Beatrice Dimmitt, but when I called her she said, "Sorry—this is out of my league. All I can suggest is contacting one of the marine societies. I think there's one up north."

"How do I get in touch with them?" I asked.

Unfortunately, Dr. Dimmitt didn't know their number. She was sympathetic, though, and promised to call back if she came up with any information. "In the meantime, sponge the dolphin with salt water to keep her from getting dehydrated. She might be able to swim out by herself at high tide."

"Thanks for the tip," I said, trying not to sound too discouraged. Hanging up the phone for a final time, I turned to Lenora, Diane, and Sonny.

"No luck?" Diane asked.

I shook my head. "I guess that first vet was right. A beached dolphin is a dead dolphin."

"Poor thing," Diane sighed. "I wonder if the baby can survive without its mother."

"I don't know," I said unhappily. "I've read some books about dolphins, but most of them discussed how they communicate and how to train them, nothing like this."

Lenora hugged me. "Don't feel so bad, honey. You tried, that's what matters. Why don't we try to forget about it—go out for ice cream or something. My treat."

"No," I told my grandmother firmly. "I

can't forget about it. Dr. Dimmitt suggested sponging the dolphin with sea water and that's exactly what I'll do, even if it means staying with her all night."

"I'll help you, Serena," Diane said.

"And so will I," Sonny said, putting his arm around me. In a low voice, for my ears alone, he added, "I care about the dolphins, Serena, but I care about you even more. And when things settle down I promise you we're going to have a serious talk. About us."

Several hours later brilliant stars dotted the evening sky and a luminous moon was rising. On my knees in the shallows, I sponged the dolphin's body. Next to me, Sonny and Diane worked quietly with sponges of their own. The three of us were like a small, determined army, all united to save one dolphin.

"What time is it now?" Diane asked for the umpteenth time.

Sonny checked his digital watch. "Nine o'clock."

"I hate to say it," I said, "but I think she's growing weaker. She's hardly moving at all."

"At least the tide is rising," Diane pointed out.

"But it may not rise soon enough," Sonny said. "You know, I've been thinking maybe we've been going about this all wrong."

"What do you mean?" I asked, dipping my sponge into the water.

"Maybe we gave up too easily. We should have kept trying to get some kind of outside help."

"But who?" Diane asked. "None of the officials in Sea Mist would help."

"Perhaps we just didn't reach the right people," Sonny said slowly. "But maybe there's a way. Hmm, I wonder if it would work. . . ." His voice trailed off, and he tossed his sponge to me. Standing up, he said briskly, "I hope you don't mind holding the fort here for a while. I've got to go somewhere."

"Where?" I asked, startled.

Sonny shook his head. "If my idea works, you'll find out soon enough. See you later."

Perplexed, I watched him start up the path.

Less than an hour had passed when I heard a shout from somewhere above me. I looked up and saw Lenora making her way cautiously down the hill. "Hiking is *not* my idea of a good time," she yelled down to me, her tone indignant. "Sonny called. He wants me to give you something."

Leaving Diane to continue sponging the dolphin, I met Lenora halfway up the hill. She was carrying a portable radio, which she handed to me.

"Why are you giving me this?" I asked.

"Just following Sonny's orders," my grandmother said, breathing hard from her exertion. "He said for you to turn it on."

"Why?"

"Listen to KNDE. That's what Sonny said," Lenora told me, following me down to the beach. "And since I'm here, you might as well hand me a sponge. I might as well be of some use."

Diane handed her Sonny's sponge while I turned on the radio and tuned it to KNDE. I nearly dropped the radio when I heard Sonny's voice on the air.

". . . KNDE listeners, I'm appealing to you. A mother dolphin has gotten tangled up in a fishing net and is beached on the shore right here in Sea Mist. Her baby is okay, but the mother is stuck, and local officials have refused to help."

Sonny went on to give the dolphin's exact

location, and asked listeners to call the station if they had any ideas, especially anyone who knew anything about dolphins.

Then just before signing off, he said something that made my heart leap with joy. "And Serena, if you're listening, I apologize for being such a coward. You know what I mean. And I want you and the entire *world* to know that you're the only girl for me!"

Chapter Twelve

Within no time at all, people started coming down the steep path to the cove, strangers and people I knew—customers of Unique Creations and even some kids from school, including several members of the girls' swim team.

A stocky, dark-haired woman hurried over to me. "You're Serena, aren't you?" she asked. "We spoke on the phone this afternoon. I'm Dr. Dimmitt. I couldn't stop thinking about what you told me—guilty conscience, I suppose. Anyway, I heard the appeal on the radio, so here I am."

Grateful for her concern, I led Dr. Dimmit

over to the beached dolphin and watched anxiously as she bent down and examined her.

When she had finished, Dr. Dimmitt said, "The sponging has helped, but we need to get her back into the water *fast.*"

I nodded, aware of the moon rising higher in the sky and making the cove almost as bright as day. Fortunately, the moon wasn't the only thing rising. The tide was, too.

From behind me a girl said, "Hi, Serena. I just got here with my boyfriend and some of his friends. Anything we can do to help?"

I turned and recognized Andrea. Tara was there, too, as well as several guys I'd seen at school. "That was some broadcast Sonny made," Tara said. She gave me a teasing grin. "And that's some boyfriend you've got, Serena!"

"It was the most romantic thing I ever heard," Andrea said dreamily. "Are you ever lucky!"

I felt a foolish smile spread across my face. Obviously Pamela had been wrong about my having no friends on the swim team. I couldn't expect everyone to like me, but at least Diane, Andrea, and Tara were real friends. Maybe some others were, too.

Realizing this healed something fragile inside me, and I was feeling pretty good when Sonny suddenly appeared next to me.

"You're back!" I cried.

"I came as fast as I could," he said, capturing my cold hand in his warm one, much as he had captured my heart. "Did you hear my broadcast?"

I nodded. "It was wonderful! *Better* than wonderful—especially the last part," I added shyly.

He brushed his lips across my forehead. "I meant every word I said."

"No matter how your father feels about it?"

"I had a talk with Dad earlier today, even before you called me on the phone. He's beginning to understand that he can't run my life for me, and I think he even respects me for it."

I smiled radiantly. "I'm so glad . . . both for you and for me!" Then I looked over at the dolphin and the swarm of concerned people milling around the cove, and my spirits fell a little. "Everything may be fine with us, but not with Twinkie's girlfriend."

Sonny pointed to the cliff where a steady stream of people was still coming down. "I think everything will be okay with her, too.

I mean, just look! There must be almost a hundred people here, and all because of my broadcast!" He grinned. "That clinches it—Dad's just going to have to get used to the fact that, for me, broadcasting is where it's at, not banking." Then he hurried off to join a group of people who were gathered around the dolphin.

Someone had brought a heavy-duty canvas tarp, and now Sonny and the others gently eased the dolphin onto it. Then they slowly waded out into deeper water, using the tarp as a makeshift stretcher, as her baby and Twinkie swam nearby. Watching the dolphins made me realize all over again how important the ocean and its creatures were to me, and how much I wanted a career in marine biology.

Everyone on the shore gasped as the female dolphin suddenly started to thrash around and made a shrill, whining sound. A hush settled over the crowd. We all strained forward to see what would happen next. The dolphin and her rescuers were now in about four feet of water. As she slid off the tarp, her baby glided up to her and nuzzled her. They exchanged squeaky, squawking noises while Twinkie swam a little farther away.

Then, flipping their tails and slicing effortlessly through the water, mother, baby, and Twinkie zigzagged out to sea together, and the crowd cheered loudly. The cove echoed with applause, whistles, and happy shouts.

Sonny's gaze met mine as he and the others sloshed back to shore, and I ran to meet him. We threw our arms around each other. Words weren't necessary—there would be plenty of time for talking later. For now, we just held each other and watched the three dolphins swim happily away.

One week later, I smiled at my reflection in the full-length mirror on my closet door. My hair was swept up on top of my head, with a few carefully arranged ringlets framing my face. I was wearing sparkly rhinestone earrings, and my satin slippers perfectly matched my beautiful party dress. Lenora had told me over and over that I looked drop-dead gorgeous, and while I wouldn't have chosen those exact words, I knew I had never looked better.

Sonny was obviously impressed when he arrived to escort me to the cotillion. His intense gaze conveyed his pleasure and approval, and the look that passed between us spoke much more clearly than words. And then, feeling like Cinderella, I went to the ball with my prince. Actually, Prince Sonny and I shared the ride with Diane and Melvin, but we might as well have been alone. They couldn't take their eyes off each other, and I had to admit that, in his tuxedo, Melvin didn't look at all like a nerd.

The evening was heavenly. Sonny's dancing instruction paid off and we danced every dance but one. That one I shared with another member of the Sinclair family—Sonny's father. No one was more surprised than I when Mr. Sinclair asked me to dance.

"Congratulations on your swimming today, Serena," he said with a warm, genuine smile as we circled the floor. "It's great for Farringdon to be number one at last. Good job!"

I smiled back, blushing. "It wasn't just me—it was a team effort."

"Modest, and pretty, too," Mr. Sinclair said with a chuckle. "I can see why my son's so taken with you. If I were a few decades younger, I just might give him some competition!"

When our dance was over, Mr. Sinclair turned me over to Sonny. I was glad when once again I was in Sonny's arms. I leaned my head against his chest and sighed happily.

"A penny for your thoughts," Sonny whispered into my ear.

"All my thoughts are of you, so they're worth a lot more than a penny," I told him. "Hundreds, thousands, *zillions* of dollars."

Sonny laughed and gently touched my lips with his. The kiss was soft, delicious, and glorious. I felt so very, very lucky! I remembered telling Diane that it would take a miracle to bring me and Sonny together, and I smiled to myself. Saving the dolphin was something of a miracle, but what Sonny and I shared was the *real* miracle. What we shared was love.